Celebrate Your Dream

Fulfill Your Destiny One Wish at a Time
A Step-by-Step Program

By

Joyce Chapman

NEW PAGE BOOKS
A division of The Career Press, Inc.
Franklin Lakes, NJ

Copyright © 2002 by Joyce Chapman

Celebrate Your Dream
Edited By Jodi Brandon
Typeset By Eileen Dow Munson
Cover design by Cheryl Cohan Finbow
Printed in the U.S.A. by Book-mart Press

To order this title, please call toll-free 1-800-CAREER-1 (NJ and Canada: 201-848-0310) to order using VISA or MasterCard, or for further information on books from Career Press.

The Career Press, Inc., 3 Tice Road, PO Box 687
Franklin Lakes, NJ 07417
www.careerpress.com
www.newpagebooks.com

Library of Congress Cataloging-in-Publication Data

Chapman, Joyce.
    Celebrate your dream : fulfill your destiny one wish at a time : a step-by-step program / by Joyce Chapman.
        p. cm.
    Includes index.
    ISBN 1-56414-563-8 (pbk.)
    1. Self-actualization (Psychology) I. Title.

    BF637.S4 .C493 2002
    158.1—dc21

                                                    2001052175

This book is dedicated to
dreamers
who are excited and
willing to claim and celebrate
their biggest dreams!

Acknowledgments

I wish to acknowledge all those dreamers who took the last page of my books, *Live Your Dream, The Live Your Dream Workbook, Journaling For Joy, Journaling For Joy ~ The Workbook, If I Had Three Wishes The Only One Would Be...,* and *If I Had Three Wishes The Only One Would Be... ~ The Workbook,* and were inspired to live life in celebration of their wishes, hopes, and dreams!

My thanks to Al Saunders, Diane Chalfant, Eldonna Lay, Eva Ditler, Gina Misiroglu, Michele Lanci-Altomare, and Sheri Matlack for the first edition of this book. Their expertise and assistance empowered me to make this work, a dream come true.

Seven years have passed since my last publication, and I now have many others to acknowledge and thank. To begin, I'd like to acknowledge and thank Nancy Reid Edwards. Nancy has been my assistant for the past several years and does a little bit of everything for and with me. With her by my side I know I will reach and celebrate my biggest dream. Thank you, Nancy!

Secondly, thanks to all the staff at Career Press/New Page Books. I sincerely know that without all your efforts I would not be writing this acknowledgment. The list of individuals who I have already been privileged to know, Ron Fry, Mike Lewis, Karen Wolf, Stacey Farkas, Jackie Michaels, Kirsten Beucler, Anne Brooks, Laurie Ann Kelly, Brenda Brienza, Brenda Conklin, Cheryl Cohan Finbow, Eileen Dow Munson, and Jodi Brandon, and I am certain that this list will grow every day and want to be sure to let them all know to write to tell me to include their names next time!

Each time I have worked with the final stages of creating a book, the individuals that I "meet" at this stage inspire me significantly. Eileen Dow Munson has added her touch to make this book as close to a work of art as typesetting and layout can produce. The cover design is often what invites a reader to be drawn to purchasing a book or workbook, and for the beautiful cover design I thank Cheryl Cohan Finbow. Working with editor Jodi Brandon has been an extraordinary experience. I know that because of her skill, expertise, and dedication to support and empower me, you will join with me to celebrate this work!

I will continue to celebrate and be thankful to all those who share and celebrate my dreams: the individuals who participated in workshops and allowed me to be their coach, as well as all my new dreamer friends I am meeting online and who filled out surveys. With your willingness to be a part of my dreams, we are able to illustrate different styles of claiming, living, and celebrating dreams!

Lastly, I thank my sons and their families: Ron, Debi, Kyle, Kasey, Deanna, Rick, Adel, Clinton, Troy, Dominique, Bobby, Ashley, and Sabrina! Standing by me and believing in the power of dreaming has sustained me through the last several years of growth and change. With their love and dedication to me, each and every day is a day of celebration!

Contents

Introduction

The idea for writing a book dedicated to achieving one's ultimate life's purpose did not come to me overnight. Although I'd like to take sole credit for having created the premise for this book in my sleep, the truth of the matter is that it was developed over many years, through living and learning from my own "life lessons," as well as those of my clients, workshop participants, family members, and friends. I developed and introduced a step-by-step plan for personal growth and reaching your ultimate dream in my first books. I knew I was inviting my readers to truly know themselves and to live life fully. As time passed, sensitive souls came to me and told me of their experiences, and of their lack of and need for an advanced road map, or set of constructive life tools, for taking what they had experienced and learned, in essence, and applying it to realize something even greater. Although many had begun their personal work, excitedly embraced their dreamwork, and felt that they were indeed living their dream, there was a real desire for something *more.* In many cases, people had simply redefined their dream, or life's course of events had naturally advanced them to another plane of living. Sometimes life just simply offers you another or often an unexpected or different path. I began to be very excited and inspired to design a new workshop to encourage the claiming of one's biggest dream and to live in the joy of celebrating each and every life event. I dared to think I could design a guide for those individuals who wanted to live their ultimate life's purpose. This book and the companion workbook are designed to be used as guides to explore that basic human traits of simply wanting to be everything that you can be and making a contribution.

This is an *advanced* course, written for those who have committed themselves to do the work required to become highly evolved students of consciousness. A structured series of exercises to begin, then maintain, upper levels of self-realization were provided in my first books, *Live Your Dream, Journaling For Joy,* and their related workbooks. Ideally my previous books have inspired new thought and led you to discover that living your dream, and writing your way to personal growth and freedom are lifelong processes.

With greater self-examination and greater self-awareness, truths are revealed. With this learning you have likely identified and realized earlier dreams. Now that you are excited and motivated to move on to bigger—and higher—dreams, you are not only ready to dedicate yourself to reaching your fullest potential, but you are passionate about claiming your destiny. Having already chosen values, beliefs, and habits that are consistent with previous dreams, you have found the joy in learning each of your life's experiences. Having worked with my (or comparable) self-help works, you have come to recognize the differences between vision and delusion, between faulty thinking, fantasy, and reality. You also know that being exposed to new ideas alone is never enough; you must acknowledge, prepare for, and work toward dreams if they are to be achieved.

This book, and its companion workbook, provide information for creating the framework you will need to discover, rediscover, identify and liberate you to then celebrate any known or hidden dream(s). Activities and assignments give you an idea about how to focus your energy to clarify your quest and help you understand that the fulfillment of your biggest dream is important to more than just you. When enough of us align with, and activate, our personal dreams, we will have a sense of greater personal fulfillment leading to creating a better world.

I applaud your readiness for this next step. I cheer your eagerness to reach your individual best. I congratulate you on your decision to accept even more of your own personal power. I rejoice in your dedication to fulfilling your destiny, and I look forward to celebrating with you as you complete each exercise in this book and in the companion workbook to rediscover the magic of living true to yourself and your dreams. I suggest that you also purchase a large art pad to provide a large enough "canvas" to plan for your biggest dream. And, as always, keep your journal close at hand, along with a selection of colored pens for adding creativity and color to liven up your pages. Exercises for you to engage in are set apart from the body of the text in italicized type.

Get ready, right now, to join with others who are stepping over the boundaries of small and ordinary thinking into higher levels of thought—that kind of innovative contemplation resulting in the design of new structures instead of patching together those that don't work anymore, and the kind of thinking that creates a new environment that nourishes our spirits instead of denying, or depleting, them. The format for turning your wishes and hopes into an attainable dream requires clarity and focus, so let us begin the process necessary to liberate, claim, and celebrate your biggest dream.

The following pages of guiding principles will serve as reminders whenever you find yourself "off course." They are outlined here in the Introduction for quick reference, but, more importantly, the book is built around these simple concepts, so that you can structure the way you approach your dreams in a way that the book is structured. In other words, if you were to hold your biggest dream up to a mirror, it would reflect back this simple process of taking your dream from concept to reality. This textbook for your "dream coursework" has a simple format: The book explores these themes one by one, provides examples of real-life people who have followed them, and suggests ways that you might implement them into your personal agenda of fulfilling your biggest dream. I encourage you to refer back to this handy synopsis every so often for a review of the principles that will assist you as you take the paths to realize your dreams.

Liberating Your Biggest Dream

You may, or may not, know what your ultimate dream is, so ask yourself the following questions: Do you find yourself hampered by the current role you are playing? Too often, we get caught up in job descriptions and roles, rather than in our missions. Have you been so busy being an entrepreneur, a friend, a caregiver, a good dad, mom, son, daughter, boss, or employee that you've suppressed or put aside what you *really* want to do? Or perhaps you've dismissed an earlier dream as adolescent, or even presumptuous. After all, how can a single person feed the world, make the planet safe for all children, establish world peace, or write an inspirational book? Have you abandoned an earlier dream because you lack the necessary credentials, or the money, or the time?

As with all your earlier journeys, this one begins with a single step. So begin the same way you began in *Live Your Dream:* by reexamining yourself and by doing all of the self-inventory work. By the end of this Introduction, you may know exactly what your next dream step is. If so, this is a wonderful place to start. You may only have a glimmer. If so, this is a wonderful place to start! Or, you may still be blocked. If so, this, too, is a wonderful place to begin. What is important is that you claim whatever you perceive your biggest dream—however fragmentary—to be at this moment.

The next step is to move forward with your dream. By doing so, you begin to step even more fully into your own personal power and ways to assume even more responsibility for that power. Next, you'll learn ways to truthfully explain to others what you are about to do, or become. Following that, you will learn ways to evaluate your progress. And, from there, you will master ways to move beyond life's challenges to become what I call a dream activator.

Getting Rid of Old Mindsets

No matter how successful we've been so far, we still carry within us old ideas, beliefs, and opinions that may no longer serve us. Indeed, those very convictions may be what will keep us from manifesting what we want most in the world. The most difficult part of identifying which beliefs are most restrictive is that we've never questioned them before. Now is the time for you to do precisely that—so that your biggest dream can become a reality.

The "Never Again" section of each chapter is designed so that you can address the specific issues that each particular chapter covers. These sections invite you to take a close look at what's been holding you back, and allow you the freedom to write about them intimately. Upon close examination, you'll probably discover that your old mindsets are so limiting, so power-draining, that they serve no purpose in fulfilling your biggest dream. Allow yourself the time to acknowledge that these mindsets exist and then release them, symbolizing a new beginning that has no room for limiting beliefs.

Claiming Your Biggest Dream

The bigger the dream, the bigger the impact. In fact, your *ultimate* dream may be far bigger than you yet realize. Acknowledge and claim as much of the dream as you know right now. By recognizing the pieces of the dream puzzle that you know, you begin the process of fulfilling your life purpose. Remind yourself to be aware of additional parts of your puzzle as they emerge. For example, if what you really want to do is make America safe for children, you may not want to limit yourself to opening one local day-care center.

For any of you who have consciously put an old dream on hold, think about those elderly adults who voice regrets for opportunities lost, or hopes unfilled. John Greenleaf Whittier perhaps best said it in his poem, "Maud Muller":

> "For of all sad words of tongue or pen
> The saddest are these: it might have been."

If you once dreamed of becoming an artist, a potter, a writer, an actor, a mother, a father, a doctor, a surgeon, a model, a professional athlete, or something no one else has dared to try yet, review that dream again. Then, don't permit yourself to be deterred by anything. Remember: There is *always* enough time and money to pursue a dream. Time and money contributing to the well-being of the planet attract additional time and money—maybe not as quickly as we'd like, but they do manifest, if only in the nick of time. The question to ask yourself if time or money is not arriving in a timely manner is this: Is my *dream big enough?* If you are in doubt, *make it bigger!* So, if you want to develop a more perfect engine or a cure for common diseases and find yourself running into block walls at every turn, *reevaluate* what you are doing and how you are doing it. Is your dream big enough? Far-reaching enough? What other options or methods might be explored? When your dream is big enough, help and helpers are waiting to be found. Just open your mind to the infinite number of resources and people available to you. Then go after them and celebrate their arrival!

The "Make the Dream Real...Make it Yours" portion of each chapter exists to help you integrate and claim your biggest dream. After finishing reading the book chapters, these sections allow you to, in essence, write your own chapter—that is, to really identify and write about what your dream means to you at that point in your journey. Through this journaling, you validate your dream and chronicle the necessary pieces of your dream in order to more fully ingrain it in your daily living, your daily walk in life, your world, and the world.

Accepting and Releasing Your Personal and Spiritual Powers

By accepting the responsibility of realizing your biggest dream, you begin to use even more of your own inner powers. Even though you have already experienced the immense growth that comes with acknowledging and using personal power, the concept of using spiritual power may make you uneasy. That's because the abuses and misuses of power are all around us. But I am not talking about power that uses or controls others. That kind of power, driven by anger, insecurity, or fear, arises when people use ego, rather than spirit, to accomplish their ends. Operating at the level of the ego, we seek to control, dominate, and manipulate to make others do our will. Although that may accomplish our ends for a time, it never lasts because no one feels safe around us. Working at the level of spirit, however, allows us to show others *by our example* that being creative, loving, intuitive, joyful, expressive, effective, responsible, independent, direct, dynamic, energetic, free, and true to who you really are stands to benefit them as well as you. Another way to explain this most vital component of personal empowerment is to realize that when we live in and from our spirit power, we energize those around us. And by energizing others, and ourselves, we are modeling and showing them how to become more of who they are. So use your powers to empower and to pass them on!

Think about the previous concepts and labels until you fully understand the difference between personal, spirit, and ego power, because the power I speak of, grounded as it is in love, is never driven by anger or insecurity. Instead, it is demonstrating and operating at the loftiest levels of the celebration of our human spirit. As such, it is refueled by the never-ending supply of energy available to us when we access our inner power and become one with the collective unconscious. In other words, the higher you elevate your thinking, the higher you raise your awareness; the more developed you become, the more you improve the world around you. The power to transform oneself is the *real* power that you seek.

As you have already discovered, once you have accepted and assimilated your power, you find yourself living in the same world, but seeing it from an entirely new position. Although old beliefs and problems may tag along, your newfound view allows you to put what you perceived as adversity into fresh perspective. Problems, then, are no longer seen as punishment, but rather as ways to continue your personal growth. A fresh perspective may be needed even as you are reading this paragraph. Just as I remind my clients, "You have the ability to leave this moment totally different from when you arrived," the same is true for you. You don't have to finish reading this paragraph with the same beliefs you held when you began. Right now, you can make the decision to become *fully* empowered, to move beyond a comfortable status quo, to gain even more control over the direction of your life, and to live in celebration. If you have been reluctant to assume more of your personal power, think about it again! Invite yourself to step into your power and celebrate your biggest dream!

Assuming Total Responsibility

Many people have confessed to having a terrific idea, only to abandon it when it began to demand commitment, to be too great of a risk, to require change or hard work, to receive a lack of support from friends and family, or to require more money. Put another way, how many dreams have *you* not yet put into action?

It's not always easy to remain enthusiastic when friends, colleagues, and family members doubt your capabilities or ideas. And a blinding flash of creativity seems less magical when years of work, research, and commitment lay ahead. Patents, lawyers, lessons, schooling, and business travel take time and money—commodities that often appear to be unavailable. Yet it is in accepting that those things are available or even possible that separates the everyday dreamer from becoming a dream activator. The people I call dream activators *do whatever needs to be done to make their dream come true!* Many dreamers often just fantasize about what would happen if their dreams came true. Without taking action, a dreamer may continue to fantasize.

Fearful of making a fool of yourself? Afraid of committing yourself to a course of action that might fail? Cautious of making uncomfortable financial moves? Of course you are; it would be irresponsible not to consider all of these things. Yet, you can't allow yourself to be immobilized by cautions that hide your dream in the shadow of your psyche. Lost or hidden dreams don't do anything for anyone. Your commitment to yourself requires that you assume total responsibility for your own progress. There is another commitment involved, too. I dedicated this book to "those eager to realize their dreams, for the future of our world requires individual fulfillment of each of our highest and noblest aspirations." Whenever you put day-to-day needs ahead of your dream, you are denying the world your measure of contribution and self-fulfillment. Remember that whenever bills become overwhelming or a forward step appears too fraught with chance. Remind yourself to pay attention to your *inner* needs. Acting upon what you discover, begin behaving as if you are already living the life you want so passionately. The life you save will be your own.

Telling Your Own Truth to Empower Your Biggest Dream

Dare to find your truth. Don't hide behind lies, deception, or denial. Never take the easy way out, telling others what you think they want to hear or what you think is acceptable or achievable. It may take some serious self-inventory work to discover your deepest desires and rediscover your primary truths.

To see, hear, and align with those truths, you must be willing to feel everything, think everything, and express everything. Let go of the fear. Don't hold back. Talk about your biggest dream. When you talk about your biggest dream, notice if censorship gets in the way. We've all been trained to be considerate, to protect others from a direct experience of our unedited opinions. But your biggest dream is not a danger to anyone else. On the contrary, living your dream frees those around you to live their own. Only when we come right out and say what we're thinking do we create an environment for change and celebration.

Forming Your Own Empowerment Team

Even if you have not fully identified your biggest dream, you probably know the direction in which you want to go. Whatever dream career you wish to be in, get yourself appropriately trained or educated and start associating with those already there! Association then provides contacts and friendships that allow you to practice living in your dream. As you move forward, affiliate yourself with people who will be traveling with you. Members of your team may include family members and old friends, fellow dreamers, mentors, advisors, and coaches.

Practicing Standing Aside

Stepping back from situations allows you to make unemotional observations, inferences, and decisions. Detach yourself from what others are doing or saying. I know what you are thinking—and you are right: It is a paradox to care with all your heart and soul about something, and then be asked to give up controlling the path! How does one practice being detached when feeling so passionately? By tapping into the universe and making decisions from your inner self. Live in the state of "Oh!" by letting go of preconceived notions of how things should be—or how they should be accomplished. Then step back and examine everything that you are doing or thinking that isn't really you. If, for instance, you still need someone else to approve or give you permission, you have not yet accepted responsibility for your own power.

If your partner, colleagues, family members, friends, or parents aren't supportive, find companions who do believe in you—and don't expose your ideas and plans to those who ridicule or doubt them. Although it would be wonderful to have those closest to you on your empowerment team, it would be unusual! Enjoy relatives and friends for who and what they are, but don't demand, or even expect, them to align with you.

Getting Through the Tough Times

Situations and events that are demanding or difficult are bound to happen when you are moving forward. When they do, reach out for assistance when you need it. Depending upon the kind of challenge or problem you encounter, choose the type of coaching/advice/expertise that will move you past the hurdle. That may be professional guidance, a friend, or time alone. It is important that you do what you need to do to learn from what is delaying your progress, and then move through—or around—it.

The most common perceived stumbling block that many adults accept is that they don't have enough money to accomplish their dreams. If you buy into that, you will not only never achieve your dreams, but you may not dare to perceive them! Take a moment to observe the world's natural abundance. You may not have tapped into as much of it as you'd like yet, but there is more than enough food, water, and shelter for you and everyone else on the planet. It is just the *distribution* of this largesse that is limited. Don't allow this notion or lack of resources limit, or stop, you from living true to your biggest dream!

Notifying Yourself and Others If Your Focus Changes

We've all lived out a life choice that turned out to be incongruent with who we thought we were—or the potential of who we could be. For that reason, I can't overemphasize the importance of being open to changing your focus or direction when needed. What is vital is admitting to yourself that you are changing direction—even if at first glance the alteration appears to indicate indecisiveness or lack of direction. Most great dreamers adapted their plans, time lines, or goals. Don't fear this! And don't regard it as some sort of failure, because it's growth in action. My way of handling this situation is to live from one of my favorite phrases: It's up to me to know what I want, and it's up to my spirit to figure out how!

Living Congruently With Your Dreams, Self, Place, Possessions, and Position

By following the principles mentioned previously, you will begin to move into the inner realm of consciousness. Rejoice by establishing a lifestyle that makes the realization of your biggest dream a top priority. That includes allowing time for inspirational thought and creative action. Spend time to be with those who nurture and empower you. At the beginning and end of each day, embrace what is and visualize what will be. Change, however unsteady, is essential, reminding you that you are alive and *growing*. So *practice* those changes that allow you to live congruently with your biggest dream.

Celebrating Your Dreams

It's your natural right to make your own life choices. By claiming the biggest dream you've chosen—by setting up your schedule to make all your dreams your top priority—you free your energy to do what you've always wanted to do. From then on you work at the jobs you really love and associate with people you really want to be around. Simply by embracing change you begin to grow. So welcome changes and start celebrating every step you accomplish, right now. Just by reading this Introduction you may have discovered or learned something about yourself that you did not know before you began.

By reading this far, you have opened yourself to a host of new ideas. Ask yourself: *Where am I in my wishes, hopes, and dreams right now? What has my dream journey been like so far? What is the greatest me I can imagine? What changes will I want to make? Am I excited to live in each moment and celebrate my existence each and every day? And what do I want to claim and discover as I read and write in this book and its companion workbook?*

Take time to ponder these questions, and record your responses on the pages that follow. You may discover (or really start to *own*) some very interesting facets of yourself and your life.

Opening the Door to a New Dream

1

If you have read my other books, you know the importance I place on dreaming dreams, achieving their fulfillment, and living from all of who you are and can be. So, what realized dreams are you celebrating right now? Celebration is the human way of savoring well-earned rewards. As a dreamer, you have dared to do something that frightened you and made earlier wishes, hopes, and dreams come true. Wasn't the sensation wonderful? And isn't it equally thrilling to know that it was through your own efforts that those dreams were manifested? Now, having become used to using your talents, gifts, and options, you can look back and see how much you influenced—perhaps even redefined—your own personal future.

There is much, much more to you than you can even imagine. Let's get in touch with that by looking ahead at your future and including into it all of your current wishes, hopes, and dreams. Pretend that you have been given an invitation to open new doors to discover your smallest and biggest dreams. What would those dreams be?

Settle back into your favorite dreaming position. Take out your favorite pen and your journal and make a list of the top 10 things you want to add to your life. Having done that, slowly and thoughtfully contemplate your dreams. Enjoy and embrace them. Then put the list where it will not be disturbed. Think about them often over the next few days. Hold them in your heart. Allow these wishes, hopes, and dreams to germinate in your mind, for this is the way to liberate your biggest dream and make it real.

For a perfect example of releasing a dream, you need to look no farther than Linda, a New York editor who was always aware of her wishes, hopes, and dreams.

Having spent years rising to the top of her profession, at 33, Linda assessed what she had accomplished and was pleased. But there were things about living and working in New York that were less than perfect. Also, in working for one company, she was restricted by the types of manuscripts she was given. On top of that, by working so hard to establish herself, she had chosen to delay marriage and a family and, biologically, time was running out. So Linda set out to redesign her life.

Her new plan included looking for a new job, one that would provide her with the time to include being a wife and mother. With an outstanding reputation established in New York, she decided to chance moving to California, where she set herself up as a freelance editor. Next on her list of "to dos" was finding a wonderful partner and having a baby. Today, five years later, she has all those things. Her freelance editing business is thriving; she is living this dream and excitedly opening new doors to new dreams.

Liberating Your Newest Dream

How wonderful it is to already have a good understanding of who and what you are. Now it is time to open the door wide on who you are, what you dare to desire, and what you can achieve! As someone who has completed earlier dreams, you no longer find it frightening to accept your own responsibility for your personal mental, physical, and spiritual growth. Yet, having accomplished that growth, you may still feel a yearning to know even more about yourself, sensing that there is something else within waiting to be released. For those with the urge to find out, not knowing strikes at your soul! If you were born to dance and have not yet embraced the performer inside, a vital part of you remains waiting in the shadows. It is time to unveil what may lie slumbering inside.

As you have learned, in the process of making any dream come true, you attract like-minded people with whom to share your ideas and goals. That process has drawn us together because my dream is to inspire and coach those willing to seek their destinies. Right now, take time to clear your mind because, despite all the work you've done to rid yourself of earlier limitations and beliefs, you still carry your history with you. Some of those memories may be holding you back from moving forward.

Start off by mentally filling a chalkboard with a list of everything standing in the way of your forward motion. Review it. Take time to record what you visualized and begin to prepare yourself for the changes that are to come—for the world depends upon the achievement of your dreams.

As an ancient Chinese proverb promises:

> If there is righteousness in the heart,
> There will be beauty in the character.
> If there is beauty in the character,
> There will be harmony in the home.
> If there is harmony in the home,
> There will be order in the nation.
> When there is order in the nation,
> There will be peace in the world.

In other words, we must not underestimate the importance of the individual—you or me or anyone else. If there is ever to be worldwide peace, it must begin within each one of us. And as we change in our view of the world, and ourselves, so do those around us. Only when we are pleased with our own progress do we freely encourage others to work toward their own fulfillment. You found this to be true while working toward earlier dreams: Your fellow dreamers, family, friends, and colleagues responded to the changes you made. Yet, here you are again, suspecting there is another—perhaps even a *bigger*—dream that will make more differences in your life and theirs! Again, maybe you have only *sensed* that biggest dream, intuitively felt it buried deep and unidentified within you. Or perhaps you have glimpsed portions of it, but have not been able to put them all together. Dreams are often akin to unassembled puzzles, and you suspect that yours is just waiting for you to put its missing sections together. Simply by embracing this awareness, you continue the journey toward discovery and accomplishment.

What's missing from your dream and celebration lists? Do you have anything you wish to add? Combine? Delete? Alter? Do that!

Consciousness as Unexplored Territory

The traveling salesman in *The Music Man* said, "You gotta know the territory!" —and he was right! Identifying a secret dream is often a journey into unknown territory because the process of finding it calls for you to consciously send your thoughts forward into uncharted terrain. Trailblazing physician Deepak Chopra states, "Consciousness is a force that most of us undervalue. Generally, we do not focus our inner awareness or use its real power, even in the most difficult moments of crisis." Even less do we value our *unconscious* mind—that personal pool of intelligence and instinct that come from a combination of the knowledge contained in our genes and life experiences. With all of the recent scientific discoveries regarding DNA, heredity, and genetic programming, why do we continue to underrate our potential? I believe we often deny our natural knowing and powers because acknowledging something of value requires that we accept total responsibility for achieving it. Rather than be held accountable for the failure or success of our desires, ambitions, and dreams, we all too often deny our ability to deliberately manifest what we want. It is, after all, much easier to blame bad luck or others for not having or becoming. To use more of our own powerful consciousness, we can access our unconscious by trusting our instincts—and our wishes and dreams. As we explore we can strengthen both through our search for knowledge, meditation, prayer, dream interpretation, journal writing, therapy, and coaching. We can then access even more energies and knowledge beyond our own genetic and experiential make-up.

This is definitely not totally new territory. Throughout the ages, creative people have tapped into the power of what Carl Jung called the "collective unconscious." I visualize the collective unconscious as an ultimate library containing all of what we already know in the universe as well as what is yet to be discovered. To reach the collective unconscious, and our highest potential, Jung said, "We must each find our own." It's a closed loop, you see; to reach ultimate knowledge, we must first develop ourselves to our fullest potential! Before we can align ourselves with this state of consciousness, we must reaffirm the power and importance of our own conscious and unconscious thoughts. Each of us, then, is an integral part of life on this planet. Therefore, it is imperative that we develop our individual talents and abilities to the fullest so that we will be ready when our biggest dreams are revealed. Consider this notion: Everyone else in the world depends upon you reaching your biggest dream if peace and harmony is to be achieved!

Does that mean that your dream must immediately and conspicuously benefit the rest of humanity? A Hebrew saying goes, "He who saves a single soul, saves the world entire!" Was it Oskar Schindler's original intent to save 1,100 Jews from death during World War II? Certainly not; he wanted to make money—lots of it! In the process of striving for his initial dream, which would only have benefited himself, he discovered a larger one. Along with it, he discovered inner strength and integrity that few had suspected. He has gone down in history as the man who saved more than a thousand Jews from certain death. Today, 11,000 descendants of those saved are alive because Schindler's original dream grew. However large your dream seems to you, it is probably bigger. Say you are dreaming of creating a loving home for your family or of inventing a more effective filing system for your office. These dreams may not immediately make life better for your neighbors or for office workers across town, yet every improvement in the world eventually benefits others. Did Henry Ford have any idea of the extent of the change he would initiate by instituting mass production of automobiles? Maybe not— but in one way or another he changed the lives of every human being on this planet! When you align yourself with the limitlessness of the universe, you will not only realize your own dream but, eventually, you will improve life for people you may never know. So, it is now time to write your story—the story of *your* dream journey so far!

Give yourself plenty of quiet time to reflect on what you have read and what you have written in your workbook and journal so far. Then, when you are ready, begin recording everything you remember about your journey so far.

By looking back at how you welcomed, approached, and achieved your previous dreams, you have opened the door to your next dreams.

Begin to think about what you are wishing, hoping, dreaming, and wanting to celebrate. Take out your pen and journal again and write about what's beyond the very next door. After you have written, reread and get ready to play "Let's imagine..." to reveal even more of what you are seeing—and what you want to see!

To actually move through each new door and beyond, you must be able to feel, taste, smell, and envision your new dreams. You've done this before, so close your eyes and make a wish. After all, wishes and hopes are the stuff that dreams are made of. The following exercise helps you start to pull all the pieces of your biggest dream together.

Take 10 minutes to clear your mind, to reopen the door to a new dream or a dream step. Take 10 minutes to gain insight, understanding, and clarity. To free yourself, to lift your spirits. To identify a block. To step into your power. To find an answer, although it doesn't need to be written in stone yet.

Take 10 minutes to invite yourself to be back in the celebration of your creative spirit.

The following writing prompts are designed to help you take exactly 10 minutes to get your life "on purpose." This exercise may be used in the following ways:

- ✧ *Close your eyes, run your fingers down the page, stop, and prepare to write using the prompt your finger lands on.*

- ✧ *Playfully let your glance fall on any one of the prompts, and write about it.*

- ✧ *Consciously select a prompt that appeals to you, or a prompt that will provide information for a challenge or issue you are dealing with, and write about it. Go down the lists, reviewing each question at a time, and answer all of them.*

- ✧ *Work with a dream partner and make up your own rules.*

Whatever method you prefer for making your selection, choose a prompt and write it at the top of a blank page, set a timer for exactly 10 minutes, and write using the following sequence of questions:

- ✧ *What is my initial, uncensored thought?*   *(3 minutes)*

- ✧ *What's holding me back?*   *(1 minute, maximum)*

- ✧ *What insight would bring me to acknowledging my biggest dream?*   *(3 minutes)*

- ✧ *After rereading what I've written, what is my specific plan for action? What will I do, and when will I have it done by? What do I want and need to write more about?*   *(3 minutes)*

The realization of a dream can only be developed within one's innermost being. The purpose behind using these prompts as idea starters is to lead yourself fully into trusting yourself, fully motivating yourself, fully recognizing yourself, and bringing your dreams into reality. For many people, this is the hardest step: Once you get to the place of knowing what you need to know, ask yourself: *Am I willing to commit and claim my dreams?*

Welcome to the promptings that may very well change your life:

- ✰ Am I a dreamer?

- ✰ What was I born to do?

- ✰ What am I here to do?

★ What am I doing to fulfill my destiny?

★ What am I doing, being, and having that are helping me to live in the excitement of realizing my biggest dream?

★ Is my current dream the "right" dream?

★ What will I have to do every moment of every day, once my dream is started in motion?

★ How will I plan a schedule for my dream?

★ What natural abilities do I have that allow for the development of my dreams?

★ What skills do I have that free me to live my dream?

★ What do I know about dreamers who have decided to live and celebrate their biggest dreams?

★ What have life's experiences taught me?

★ What rumors do I want to hear about myself celebrating my biggest dream?

★ What is the biggest dream I have realized to date?

★ How did I celebrate the realization of my biggest dream to date?

★ What smaller dreams have I reawakened by claiming my biggest dream?

★ What are the stages of my dreamer self?

★ What belief statements empower me?

★ In what situations do I take risks?

★ In what situations do I hesitate to take risks?

★ What do I have to do to become an actualized dreamer?

★ What do I need to go beyond to become an actualized dreamer?

★ What path is mine to choose?

★ Am I having fun yet?

★ Who do I need to surround myself with so that my dream is possible?

★ Is the work I now engage in bringing me the money I need and want?

★ Am I practicing what would allow me to have my biggest impact on the world?

★ What did I do today to prevent myself from living my dream?

★ What happened in my life yesterday that taught me something?

★ What am I doing today to apply the lessons I learned from yesterday?

★ Is realizing my dream worth changing for?

★ What do I want and need to value today, this week, this month, and this year?

★ What stretch do I need to turn my dream into a reality?

★ Am I taking full responsibility for the realization of my dream?

★ If I had just arrived on the planet and my job was to teach others to dream, what would I teach them? What would my plan be?

★ In what ways can I contribute to the lives of others?

★ What did I do, or can I do, to enhance and enrich someone's life today?

★ What should definitely be on my schedule today?

★ What am I going to need on my journey? (Expand upon the idea of going on this adventure with everything I think I need and want to travel on this dream journey.)

★ Do I want to reclaim any of my shattered dreams, or claim any dreams left by the wayside?

★ Who am I?

★ What stories have I collected on my way to realizing my big dream? (Make a list of story titles. Choose one of these stories to write, and then share it with someone.)

★ What are the stages of my claiming my power?

★ What are 50 ways I celebrate my power.

★ Have I lost my power?

★ Do I have a spirit of liberation?

✸ Am I feeling powerful?

✸ Am I looking powerful?

✸ What needs to be released in order for me to step into my power?

✸ What secrets am I keeping from myself?

✸ Is it hard work to realize my potential?

✸ Am I willing to do the work necessary to realize my potential? If so, use the following suggestions will help you further explore and gain new insight.

   ✧ Write 10 affirmations that will empower you to embark upon your biggest dream.

   ✧ Write 25 beliefs that will empower you.

   ✧ Write a letter to someone from your past and tell him or her what your biggest dream is. Convince the person that you have no doubt you will succeed.

   ✧ List ways to make your dream known.

   ✧ Write your job description.

   ✧ Make a list of outrageous accomplishments you already achieved.

   ✧ Make a list of shattered dreams.

   ✧ Make a list of unclaimed dreams.

   ✧ List the ways in which stepping into your dream empowers you.

✸ What's next?

Never Again

Never again do you need to resist or doubt your learning!

Now that you've completed this chapter, you'll never again have to be afraid to open the door to any new dream. By integrating the learning from this first chapter, you've given yourself permission to be a dream activator. Right here—right now—address this notion to reaffirm your willingness to embrace your biggest dream. As you work through the "Never Again" section of each chapter, you are putting old ways behind you and claiming the new.

Write about what you've read and written so far that helped you or will help open new doors.

_____

_____

_____

_____

_____

_____

_____

_____

_____

_____

_____

_____

_____

_____

_____

_____

_____

_____

_____

_____

_____

_____

_____

_____

_____

_____

_____

List current and remembered information and ideas that have helped, empowered, and inspired you to continue your journey of living true to yourself and your dreams.

List anything and everything that has shaped and helped develop your sense of self.

_____

_____

_____

_____

_____

_____

_____

_____

_____

_____

_____

_____

_____

_____

_____

_____

_____

_____

_____

_____

_____

_____

_____

_____

_____

_____

_____

_____

_____

List life experiences, plays, films, books, and so on that have reminded and inspired you that you are able to attain any dream.

_____

_____

_____

_____

_____

_____

_____

_____

_____

_____

_____

_____

_____

_____

_____

_____

_____

_____

_____

_____

_____

_____

_____

_____

_____

_____

_____

_____

_____

_____

_____

_____

Write about the real and fictional people who have influenced you to strive to reach your destiny. Define in tangible terms what these people have "given" you, whether they be character traits, words of wisdom, hope, enlightenment, inspiration, encouragement, or gifts.

_____

_____

_____

_____

_____

_____

_____

_____

_____

_____

_____

_____

_____

_____

_____

_____

_____

_____

_____

_____

_____

_____

_____

_____

_____

Record any personal revelations that might still need investigating.

_____

_____

_____

_____

_____

_____

_____

_____

_____

_____

_____

_____

_____

_____

_____

_____

_____

_____

_____

_____

_____

_____

_____

_____

_____

_____

_____

_____

Now you are better able to accept the responsibility of making your dream a reality. It will be most valuable for you to continue doing this in a highly visual way. As Shakespeare wrote, "All the world is a stage," and you are now coming up out of the audience to take your rightful place. On a stage of your own making. In later chapters, you will be writing the script that you want to follow.

In the space that follows, make a cluster design of all that you want in your life, starting right now.

Whatever you are aware of you can incorporate into your life. In the Introduction, 12 basic guidelines were introduced to direct you toward fulfillment. Addressing and understanding each will let you know if you are ready and willing to make the changes today that will make realizing your biggest dream possible.

Although you may or may not know what your biggest dream is, you now understand that, like all journeys, this one begins with a single step. By reexamining yourself, you have discovered much that you did know— and maybe more that you were not consciously aware of. From this you have grown in your perception of yourself. You also recognize the importance of never underestimating the role you play in the universal scheme of things. Then, too, you have likely identified some of the things that have stood in the way of opening the door to your dream. So even if your biggest dream is not fully identified, or your journey fully planned, now is time to start moving onward.

Set aside plenty of time to write about what all this means to you.

_____

_____

_____

_____

_____

_____

_____

_____

_____

_____

_____

_____

_____

_____

_____

_____

_____

_____

_____

_____

_____

_____

_____

_____

_____

_____

_____

_____

_____

_____

_____

_____

_____

_____

Do you know your biggest dream—your destiny?

_____

Are you willing to do the work required to realize your potential?

_____

Are you willing to make necessary changes in life and in yourself?

_____

What immediate changes are you willing to make?

_____

_____

_____

_____

_____

_____

_____

_____

_____

_____

_____

_____

_____

_____

_____

_____

_____

_____

_____

_____

_____

_____

_____

_____

_____

_____

_____

_____

_____

_____

Write about what other changes will need to be made to make your smallest and biggest dreams come true.

_____

_____

_____

_____

_____

_____

_____

_____

_____

_____

_____

_____

_____

_____

_____

_____

_____

_____

_____

_____

_____

_____

_____

_____

_____

_____

Write a letter to me, or a dreamer friend, to share what you have to do to set the liberation of your biggest dream in motion.

_____

_____

_____

_____

_____

_____

_____

_____

_____

_____

_____

_____

_____

_____

_____

_____

_____

_____

_____

_____

_____

_____

_____

_____

_____

_____

_____

_____

_____

_____

_____

_____

_____

Write about why you are willing to make each of these changes.

_____

_____

_____

_____

_____

_____

_____

_____

_____

_____

_____

_____

_____

_____

_____

_____

_____

_____

_____

_____

_____

_____

_____

_____

_____

_____

_____

_____

_____

Make the Dream Real...Make it Yours

To instill the reality of your biggest dream in your subconscious as well as your conscious mind, address the following even though they may appear repetitive. Writing your thoughts and feelings down creates a greater awareness and often makes them more real. It also allows you to carry them with you. On the following pages write your declarations. After you've completed the following pages, you may want to copy them and take them with you wherever you go. Hang your lists in your office space on a bulletin board as reminders and for inspiration.

Write about what liberating your biggest dream means.

_____

_____

_____

_____

_____

_____

_____

_____

_____

_____

_____

_____

_____

_____

_____

_____

_____

_____

_____

_____

_____

_____

_____

Write about what, at this point, you understand your biggest dream to be.

_____

_____

_____

_____

_____

_____

_____

_____

_____

_____

_____

_____

_____

_____

_____

_____

_____

_____

_____

_____

_____

_____

_____

_____

_____

_____

_____

Why do you want to realize your fullest potential?

_____

_____

_____

_____

_____

_____

_____

_____

_____

_____

_____

_____

_____

_____

_____

_____

_____

_____

_____

_____

_____

_____

_____

_____

_____

_____

_____

_____

The changes you are willing to make in yourself will alter your life in many ways. Describe how.

_____

_____

_____

_____

_____

_____

_____

_____

_____

_____

_____

_____

_____

_____

_____

_____

_____

_____

_____

_____

_____

_____

_____

_____

_____

_____

_____

_____

_____

_____

What are the changes you are willing to make in your present situation?

_____

_____

_____

_____

_____

_____

_____

_____

_____

_____

_____

_____

_____

_____

_____

_____

_____

_____

_____

_____

_____

_____

_____

_____

_____

_____

_____

Rejoice!

By claiming all your wishes, hopes, and dreams, you are making them real. Having made these commitments to yourself, you are becoming a new person. You can never return to who you were before. Therefore, what you have written reflects who and where you are right now.

Breaking Free of Old Mindsets

2

Welcome to the world of new ideas; yours are among them!

Before you can go on to develop your thoughts and plans to their fullest, you will probably need to get rid of a number of unsuspected old ideas, habits, and attitudes blocking your way. For instance, have you ever noticed how much each of us focuses on problems? No matter where you turn, friends, newscasters, and reporters are discussing difficulties with personal issues, health care, immigration, crime, disease, and national and international debt. Yet, despite our concern—and all the brainpower being devoted to solving these problems—world difficulties are still very evident. Each of us can easily become overwhelmed by the amount of "fixing" there is to do out there.

Well, the best solution may not be to fix broken relationships, dysfunctional systems, waste, greed, or lack of common sense, although many are trying to do so. The solution to old problems lies in developing new ideas, some based upon the successes and failures of the past and others based upon an entirely new vision or fresh perspectives. In new approaches are opportunities to develop workable procedures and prototypes. This is where you come in, because we can no longer continue to use old methods and materials—however successful they may have been in the past.

Each of us needs to observe old and new problems from entirely different points of view and become creative.

Examining Old Mindsets

Every day, someone accomplishes the inconceivable. Severely injured, a professional skier needed to recover completely before heading back into competition. Although she was physically healed, she knew that she had to do more than just repeat earlier performances. This time, she had to conquer fears that she'd never had before the accident. That meant, in order to return to serious competition, she would also have to move *beyond* old limitations established by previous successes. How does an athlete move beyond mental limitations of prior wins? She did it by creating an *entirely* new experience: by going skydiving! Then, having viewed the mountain from a whole new perspective, she was able to confidently compete again. Although she didn't win her next race, she took a quantum leap in preparing for her next race—and the one after that.

Take a minute right now to ask yourself: What restricting ideas or mindsets are holding me back? The world's present understanding of quantum physics—our current belief that nothing is faster than the speed of light? That for every winner there must be at least one loser? That I'm too inexperienced? I'm too old? I'm not important enough for important people to listen to me? Well, guess what: None of those beliefs may be valid!

Years ago, no one outside San Diego, California had ever heard of me, but I knew that what I had learned could inspire and improve people's lives. Despite never having written a book, without owning a word processor or computer (I don't even type well—but I dictate real well!), and without knowing one thing about writing or publishing, I wrote a book, had it published, and then wrote a second book and had *it* published. Then the first edition of this book was published, along with companion workbooks for all three. Who was I? No one known well enough to be considered important! How did I do it? By constantly working toward my own highest development, which started with going back to school, as I continued teaching and then began to create and develop new programs. If I can do it, you can claim and achieve your dreams, too!

Embracing New Viewpoints

Each of us is confronted from time to time with small and/or big portions of ourselves that no longer function as well as we'd like. What that tells us is that it is time to find new ways of doing things. To identify those malfunctioning, or outgrown, parts of ourselves that need to be replaced, we need to take another look back to see how we were influenced in the past. That's because we are sometimes acting and living from that which we don't even realize hampers us and stops us from living from joy and in celebration. Often, that "stuff" is the result of a single event or comment. Now is the time to reevaluate what needs to be let go of and establish a new framework for our dreams and ourselves.

Ellie, one of my clients, reviewed a list I compiled of beliefs and feelings established in childhood that can influence our adult lives. Ellie reported that days later a thought surfaced. "It seemed to rise right out of my right shoulder," she said. "And it traveled up over my head and announced, 'Boys always win!' Now, where the hell did that come from?" she asked. The answer to her question arrived while she was dreaming a few nights later.

Ellie dreamed she was back in junior high, being approached by female teachers who were urging her to run for school president against the most popular and intelligent boy in eighth grade. "We want you to give Jim a run for his money," they said. Had Ellie been more aware, she might have heard the disclaimer: Her teachers had no hope that she would win—only that she would "give Jim a run for his money." Confidently, she enlisted friends, made dozens of posters, prepared and gave her speech, and lost the election.

Had she been hurt? I asked her. No.

Had she been angry? No.

I asked her if she remembered how she had felt. "I had been surprised," she answered. "Mystified! I'd never lost anything before. And how could I lose when I'd committed myself so completely, and worked so hard to win?" But "before" had been in elementary school. In factory towns of the 1950s, different rules applied for teenagers and adults. From junior high on up, tradition dictated that boys hold all-important offices, except secretary. Secretaries were always girls.

"So," I asked. "How has the belief that boys always win restricted you?" She wasn't sure. In the days that followed, Ellie found her thoughts returning to that question again and again. During our next visit, she observed that she had frequently been asked to run for public office. Always, she had refused; the last thing she wanted or needed, she believed, was to compete in a public arena. Yet she willingly designed brochures and worked for supervisory, mayoral, and school-board candidates. In addition to being an educator, she was an author and a museum curator. But *run for office?* Absolutely not!

"What are you going to do the next time you are asked?" I questioned.

"Well, we'll never know," she laughed. "I'm too old, and we live in the county. There are few public offices in a county system!" You can imagine her surprise when she was asked, only weeks later, to assume a recently vacated seat on a county planning group. Totally committed to getting beyond the old mindset that had, until now, kept her from fulfilling her potential, Ellie accepted. In the next election her name will be on the ballot when she runs for the seat. Already, she has been assured that she will be supported by prestigious homeowners groups and political factions. Where is all this going? Ellie doesn't have the vaguest idea. She only feels that she must do this, even though it is stepping into a void she has avoided for more than 40 years. What old "can't" or "not" is holding you back? Isn't it time to take a new look at the situation? Once these old unconscious limitations have been examined and reassessed, each of us can then *consciously* decide to change direction and take charge to create an exciting future.

Finding the Flaw

When my children were younger, I sewed a great deal, partly due to necessity, and partly because I truly enjoyed the piece-by-piece, stitch-by-stitch routine after dealing with my rambunctious children all day. At times, just as I was finishing a project, I would discover that I'd failed to do something right. Dealing with a flawed garment—or a flawed dream—can be more than discouraging; sometimes it is fatal to the whole process. That's why it is necessary to do a step-by-step reevaluation of all the leftover "can'ts" and "nots" that might be around.

Try this experiment: On the large art pad I suggested you buy, make a cluster diagram of everything that might be holding you back from pursuing your dream.

Identifying your old restrictions and writing them down on paper makes it easier to see earlier decisions that you have come to regret or question. When you have identified all the limiting factors that you know, look them over to see if anything is missing. By recognizing what is in your way, you can attend to it. You might want to include the following in your diagram: adequate financing, unresolved issues, family members, friends, coworkers, fellow dreamers, inadequate preparation, incomplete accreditation, lack of self-awareness, fear of success, and making wrong choices.

On page 59 is an example of a cluster diagram one of my clients made.

Old goals

Old restrictions

Old patterns

Old wishes

Old desires

Old relationships

Old problems

Old weak points

Old limitations

Old focus

Old lifestyles

Old thinking

Old methods of release

Old attitudes

Old traditions

Old habits

Old objectives

Old drama

Old challenges

Old dreams

Old beliefs

The past

Old excuses

Old attachments

Old frustrations

Select one particular area that you want to examine more closely. For example, consider "old attitudes." Using this as a focus, create a second cluster diagram that helps you more specifically identify what your old attitudes are. Here's a sample:

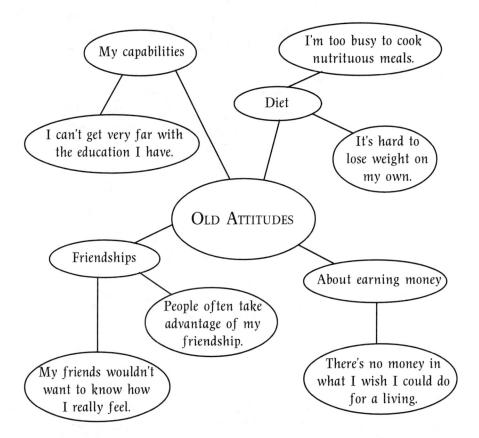

If you listed "fear of not having adequate financing" as an old attitude, for example, you can clarify it by recalling when you first experienced not having enough money. Were you 9 years old and fearful that you wouldn't have enough to get into a movie? Did you worry that you might not have enough money to buy your mother something for Mother's Day? On a first date, when you worried that your date might order too much food?

Or was it when your parents couldn't afford to pay for something you really wanted? Follow your feelings of fear back to their beginnings. Remember what you did to get beyond the fear that time. What can you do to get beyond it this time? You can't, after all, allow old fears to limit you now—not if you have decided to claim, live, and celebrate your dreams!

Having completed this second diagram, you can view some of the notions that may be holding you back. Now you can consciously choose to release limiting ideas and conditions. But you must first replace them from a totally new viewpoint.

To do that, make a third diagram. In it, select new attitudes to replace each of your former beliefs in the second diagram. Remember: You are viewing old limitations in an entirely new way. Revisit each remembered former belief or attitude and begin to redesign from a completely new vantage point. Here's an example:

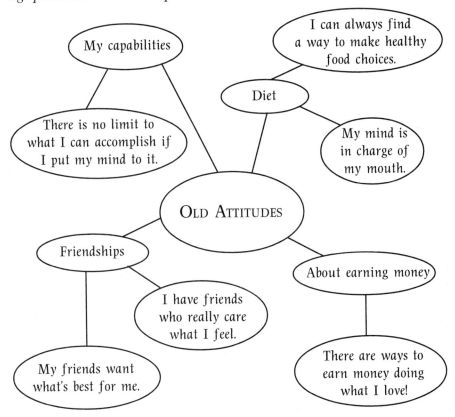

By using this identification-and-replacement technique, you break through each of those barriers keeping you from using your full power to accomplish what you want. Congratulate yourself, and expect unexpected shifts in your everyday understanding of "the way things ought to be" to emerge—the result of casting light into your mind's previously shadowed nooks and corners. By consciously exposing outdated constraints, you begin to release the power to create your biggest dreams. But is there another piece of the puzzle?

Imagine that you have in front of you the pieces of a puzzle that illustrate all the wishes and dreams that you have already realized. Draw a similar puzzle on your art pad. Leave one puzzle piece blank, and label the rest with your realized dreams. Here's an example that one of my clients drew:

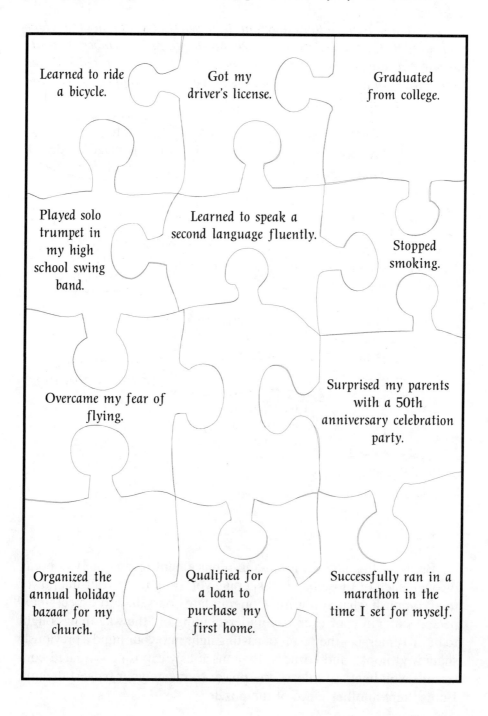

Learned to ride a bicycle.

Got my driver's license.

Graduated from college.

Played solo trumpet in my high school swing band.

Learned to speak a second language fluently.

Stopped smoking.

Overcame my fear of flying.

Surprised my parents with a 50th anniversary celebration party.

Organized the annual holiday bazaar for my church.

Qualified for a loan to purchase my first home.

Successfully ran in a marathon in the time I set for myself.

Examine those pieces and acknowledge yourself! What process did you go through to complete those dreams? Isn't it interesting how, although they are separate and distinct in themselves, they fit together? How did each dream relate to the others: Sequentially? Independently? Does that suggest anything about the unlabeled piece of the puzzle? What newly realized dream do you think you want to put there?

Now, once again review your puzzle and write in the blank puzzle piece what you want to experience to complete your current dream puzzle.

Whether or not you have identified your next dream, recognize and acknowledge the joys that you have already experienced. Reflection and review are always helpful when embracing new dreams and facing or experiencing challenges. As are life and learning, reflection and review are ongoing processes. In other words, repetition is essential for growth. Repeat these exercises as often as you need, just as you play and replay your favorite music, reread your favorite books, or watch your favorite movies for the umpteenth time. Everything that we love can be revisited and reviewed so that we might reacquaint ourselves with beauty, happiness, joy, and celebration—and so that we might be alerted to any nuances we might have missed.

Moving Beyond Perceived Limitations

We cannot allow ourselves to limit our dreams based upon past experiences—negative *or* positive. Even those of us who think we have worked through earlier obstacles often retain vestiges of old hurts and failures. You may have attained many of your dreams by healing some of those wounds: coming from a dysfunctional family, living in poverty, or simply having had little or no opportunity to be powerful. Knowing, as an adult, that it was your *choice* to either dwell in days gone by or use those experiences to grow and expand, you chose to grow. However, even if your parents merely quenched your investigative spirit, you may have some ghost messages to remove from your unconscious, questions or statements such as, "Who do you think you are…

* ☆ Queen of Sheba?"
* ☆ King of Siam?"
* ☆ God's gift to women?"
* ☆ Mrs. Got Rocks?"

* ☆ Mr. Big Shot?"
* ☆ Little Miss Know-It-All?"
* ☆ Miss Goody Two-Shoes?"
* ☆ Mr. Wonderful?"

* ☆ A Dreamer?"

Were you told that dreamers never accomplished anything? That if you were going to get anywhere it was time to pull your head out of the clouds? Were you told that only fools look for pie in the sky?

As a child, it is unlikely that you replied, "Why, yes, that's absolutely right: I *am* the Queen of Sheba," but you can now. You can say, *I do know what I want. I am a dreamer, and dreamers are perfectly capable of keeping their feet on the ground while their heads are in the clouds! As a dreamer, I am* supposed *to beat my own drum in a rhythm all my own!*

Take time right now to make a list of every limiting statement you have ever been told. Include all the messages you've ever received about what you can't possibly do or become. When you finish, go back and underline the statements you heard that stopped you in your tracks. If other forgotten messages surface later, be sure to add them to your list so that you will be aware of them and will not allow them to limit you again.

Although those limitations are an important chapter in your book of life, embrace them and be ready to live and celebrate your dreams. Never deny what's gotten you to this point, but allowing what no longer "fits" will influence your decisions can diminish your forward movement, if you allow it to do so. Instead, embrace your history. Build strength in your broken parts. Then, step aside and move on! And from now on, when someone asks you the equivalent of "Who do you think you are:_____?" answer firmly:

> I'm a dreamer. Before anything becomes reality, the idea must be born. And I dream wonderful things and commit myself to work creatively toward bringing all my dreams into reality for the benefit of us all!

By doing this, you give yourself permission to change. In not permitting that change, we limit ourselves with someone else's beliefs. Akin to domestic elephants, we continue to be inhibited by early training. Baby elephants held in captivity, as you may know, are often chained by one leg to a stake that allows them only a fixed range of movement. Even when the connecting chain is removed, the metal anklet that remains prevents them from knowing they are free. Too often, we accept parameters established for us by authority figures in our childhood.

Within days of entering preschool or kindergarten, most of us gave up a good measure of our natural spontaneity, energy, and drive. "Don't daydream," you were told, teaching you that paying attention to authority is far more important than dreaming. Then you learned the importance of sitting quietly in your seat, getting permission to go to the bathroom, and walking, not running, in the hall. It didn't take you long to learn the advantages of earning the teacher's goodwill, and soon you were spending most of your energy becoming an adult's definition of a "good" boy or girl. Certainly some limitations are necessary for every child as he or she grows into adulthood, but the truth is that the main reason that most children are stripped of their instinctive energy and enthusiasm is that most adults don't believe that individual vigor or power is convenient—or even possible—for ordinary *people.* So we often grow up thinking it is more desirable to be popular with friends and approved of by "higher-ups" than to reactivate our natural power. Then, to make sure that our children are as successful as we are, we require the same compromising things of them that were required of us. Begin to imagine a world where being totally true to oneself and one's dreams is nurtured and encouraged.

Untying the Knots of Forgotten Perceptions

As a former teacher, a mother, and a grandmother, I confess that life is quieter and more orderly when we subdue the natural instincts of children. But, oh, what we lose when we suppress a child's spontaneous delight in learning.

Adults lose by not realizing that they need to reclaim their natural power when they grow up. In part, that is because the limitations we have lived with have become so comfortable that we sometimes forget that we've outgrown them. We don't know that, once again, we can trust ourselves to express who we really are. In forgetting, we have denied ourselves the thrill of exploration and discovery, the satisfaction of growth, and the joy of celebrating the appropriate uses of power.

But, you say, *I understand all of that, and I am still feeling reluctant. Maybe because the size of this new dream is intimidating.* If your dream is large, then it is possible that the reluctance you feel is a result of some old "nots."

The "nots" that you accept may be so firmly embedded in your thinking process that you've never questioned them. Those "nots" cause anxiety. They drain your energy. They sabotage your progress. Think of these "nots" as knots. Just as you can't jump a knotted rope, or fashion an attractive bow from twisted ribbon, you can't be your most *powerful* self if you are knotting up your own creative flow! Here is a list to consider—it may lead you to discover just how your perceptions might be obstructing your progress.

Notice what each phrase "says" to you, and when one describes you, circle it:

◇ Not passionate.

◇ Pretending not to know.

◇ Not loving.

◇ Not working.

◇ Not taking responsibility.

◇ Not prepared.

◇ Not knowing.

◇ Not risking.

◇ Not enough time.

◇ Not willing.

◇ Not changing.

◇ Not taking action.

◇ Not fit enough.

◇ Not learning.

◇ Not taking time.

◇ Not prepared.

◇ Not celebrating.

◇ Not enough energy.

◇ Not capable.

◇ Not smart enough.

◇ Not nice enough.

◇ Not right.

◇ Not interested.

◇ Not talented.

◇ Not polite.

◇ Not educated enough.

◇ Not pretty/handsome.

◇ Not safe.

◇ Not doing what makes my heart sing/spirit fly.

◇ Not a priority.

◇ Not important.

◇ Not significant.

◇ Not fun.

◇ Not focused.

◇ Not efficient.

◇ Not assertive.

◇ Not tough enough.

◇ Not tactful.

◇ Not effective.

◇ Not rich enough.

◇ Not cultured enough.

◇ Not understanding.

◇ Not good enough.

◇ Not neat enough.

◇ Not organized.

◇ Not thin enough.

◇ Not experienced.

◇ Not valuable.

◇ Not worthy.

◇ Not enough encouragement.

❖Not reaching out.

❖Not enough money.

❖Not enough money to learn.

❖Not telling the truth.

❖Not practicing what I know.

❖Not enough money to celebrate.

❖Not confident.

❖Not exciting.

❖Not in a good mood (or good enough mood).

❖Not happy enough.

❖Not choosing to be with other celebrants and dreamers.

❖Not dreaming my biggest dream.

(Add your own personal" nots.")

Not _____ .

Not _____ .

Not _____ .

Not _____ .

Not _____ .

Not _____ .

Not _____ .

Not _____ .

Not _____ .

Not _____ .

Not _____ .

Not _____ .

Make a copy of the list with your "nots" circled and post it where you will see it every day. When you identify any additional "nots," add them to your list. Then note in your companion workbook, journal, or pad of paper, those changes you can make to start untangling those knots. Describe how you can begin making those changes that allow you to activate your dreams by pulling you closer to the position in which you belong.

Liberating Your Limitations

For example, if you are "not happy," break free from that limitation by writing about what it feels like to be happy!

Right now, grab your journal and make a list of times when you have been happy. Then reread and write in more detail about those experiences and what it would take for you to be happy right now. Specify where that happiness could lead you. List your options to reach that place. Determine what would free you to do what you need to do. Write down what you need in order to make that a reality. You might also find or draw a picture of yourself that captures you being happy and frame or paste it into your journal.

This process jump-starts you out of the "nots." Removing one of these blocks can be thought of as opening the floodgates of a dam. Suddenly, your life has the freedom to surge ahead. Do you feel that emancipation? Reviewing the phrases in the previous section and then writing in your journal will very likely jump-start you out of your "nots." Say, for instance, that you cannot get beyond "not in a good/good enough mood." What worked in the past to lift you out of a bad mood? Did you feel it dissipating by taking a walk, watching a sunrise or sunset, exercising, lighting a candle, listening to music, soaking in a tub of hot water, getting a massage, or talking with a friend or your coach?

List those things you've practiced in the past. Review your list and choose one to review and to activate—right now!

Say that you circled, for example, "not risking." Remember the successful risks you have already taken? Think about the growth you made by taking them. Now, consider your next risky steps.

Make a list of those next risky steps and encourage yourself to acknowledge your willingness to make those steps successful, too.

What if you identified "not telling the truth"? First, figure out if you've been hanging onto faulty thinking. As an adult you might find that the "rules" you accepted as a child are now merely a child's perception of an adult situation or attitude.

List those long-held "nots." Ask yourself: What is true for me right now?

If you identified "not enough money" as the reason for not following your dreams, listen to yourself. Trust the messages your subconscious mind gives you. You might now realize it may be time to reexamine your money beliefs, habits, and attitudes.

If you listed "not changing" as one of your "nots" and you know that change was—and is—necessary, trust that it is time to move forward. In other words, stop waiting; begin making those small and large changes that add up to important progress.

Make a list of your new guidelines and beliefs.

Having completed, and contemplated, the preceding exercises, know that you are moving right along. But be watchful as you continue along your way. Be on the alert for the "not" traps that would pull you away from your destination. Catch yourself whenever you even suspect a "not." Then be awake and aware and choose to change.

Each time you recognize and avoid a "not," record what you did to circumvent it and how it kept your forward motion intact. Make a record of those experiences. In each case, chronicle how you experienced your power, and how you expressed it. Untying, or going beyond, the knots is not a one-time exercise, so use those successful situations to guide you beyond those "nots" in the future.

Accepting No Limits: Think Big!

Know that you are a transformative force in this interconnected world and accept no limits to what you can be or contribute. Elevate your thinking by considering some of the most far-reaching dreams in human history. And remember: Most started as a dream: the Pyramids; elaborate canal systems in ancient China, Egypt, and 19th-century New York state; the Sistine Chapel; Beethoven's *Ninth Symphony*; the cotton gin; electricity; the combustion engine; automobiles; flight; wonder drugs; television; telephones; Disneyland; computers; the Internet; and so on. Daily, new ideas, products, and services astonish us. What hasn't changed enough in history is the way individuals and nations perceive one another; we still see each other as "them" and "us." Many businesses and governmental structures haven't changed either; nor the view that for every winner there must be a loser or that military forces are for conquering and controlling rather than actively teaching and illustrating the principles of democracy and fairness. Of course, that would require that *all* military forces be formally instructed in the ideals of democratic process. Many are unlikely to change their views, but there is hope for new viewpoints.

Yet, just for fun, let's go straight for world-shaking results by doing the following exercise.

Take a blank piece of paper and title it "Pie-in-the-Sky Dreams." Draw the outlines of clouds over the entire page. Inside each cloud write in some of the ingenious inventions, concepts, and discoveries that have been accomplished to date. Do you identify with any of them? Remember this! An example is shown on page 70.

Pie-in-the-Sky Dreams

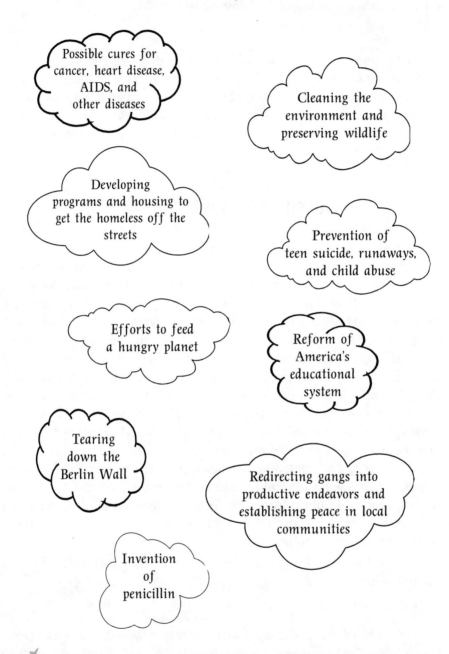

Possible cures for
cancer, heart disease,
AIDS, and
other diseases

Cleaning the
environment and
preserving wildlife

Developing
programs and housing to
get the homeless off the
streets

Prevention of
teen suicide, runaways,
and child abuse

Efforts to feed
a hungry planet

Reform of
America's
educational
system

Tearing
down the
Berlin Wall

Redirecting gangs into
productive endeavors and
establishing peace in local
communities

Invention
of
penicillin

Go deep into your inner knowing self to lift your dreams and thoughts higher. Ask: Why am I here on this planet at this time in history? What was I born to create—or continue? What am I going to create as my legacy?

On another page write the title "My Pie-in-the-Sky Dreams." Draw at least 12 clouds. Inside each one, write an idea that can change the world. Again, here's an example from one of my clients:

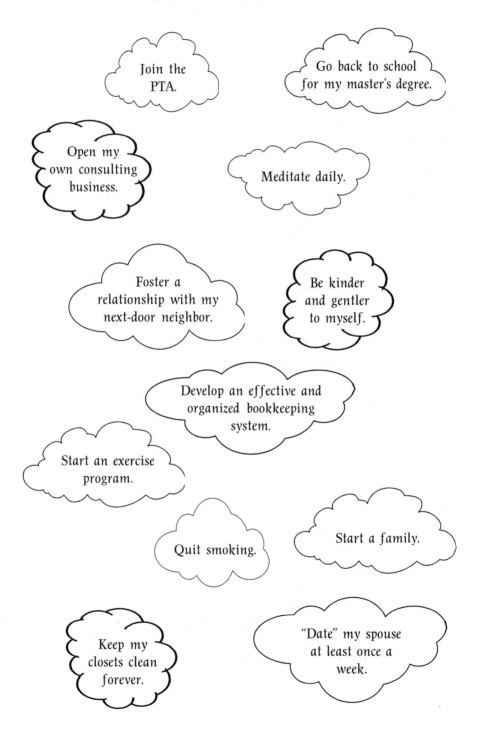

As you recorded your "pie-in-the-sky" dreams, did you go back to a particular moment in time when, for you, they were still very real possibilities? How do they correspond to the dreams you have already accomplished? How do they relate to the dreams you are working on now? Did you include your biggest dream?

If you are finding this exercise difficult, put your pen down and recall all the wishes, hopes, and dreams you ever had. Should you need to be reminded or inspired, remember those television programs or articles that continue to demand your attention. What is it about those situations or subjects that appeal to you? Do you love old movies? Is it the actor or the story that captures you? Does any particular movie have anything to do with an old dream? What about developments in genetics or negotiations between warring tribes, clans, or countries? Write down anything that comes to mind. Then, when you've dredged up all that you can, look at what you've written and imagine an inner voice saying, "Not big enough—go beyond. Dream bigger! A lot bigger!" Finish this sentence in your journal: The biggest dream I am claiming at this moment is....

Moving Forward, Growing, and Expanding

Vow to do whatever it takes to lift yourself above the mundane activities and thoughts of your everyday world. Having already scheduled time for inspirational thought, you can now sit back in a favorite place and begin thinking about where you are going. With your eyes closed, you begin raising your consciousness, lifting your inner self higher than your past, higher than your current reality. Then, soaring in a creative space, you observe that the future you want belongs to you and you alone. No one before or after you will inhabit that space. The realization that you and your contributions are important—that without you and what only you can do, a vital part of the universe may collapse and die. Comprehending this, you feel a sense of wonder; everything that you are now and ever will be starts here—beyond the perceived confines of what most people believe. You realize that you can accomplish what needs to be done because not any one of us works alone. When we are working with clarity of purpose, we work with a higher purpose and the more concentrated energy of the universe. Without all those perceptions restricting you, you can move forward into a fuller expression of your powers.

Never Again

Now that you have completed this chapter, you'll never again have to be restricted by old mindsets. However you *do* have to take care not to fall back into outgrown patterns when facing the unfamiliar. Right here—right now—reflect, review, and write so that you may forever live in choice!

What have you written and read that helped you break free of old mindsets?

_____

_____

_____

_____

_____

_____

_____

_____

_____

_____

_____

_____

_____

_____

_____

_____

_____

_____

_____

_____

_____

_____

What have you observed recently and in the past that helped empower you to identify and break free of old mindsets?

_____

_____

_____

_____

_____

_____

_____

_____

_____

_____

_____

_____

_____

_____

_____

_____

_____

_____

_____

_____

_____

_____

_____

_____

_____

_____

List the books, people, research, and radio and television programs that invited you to examine your thinking and your choices.

_____

_____

_____

_____

_____

_____

_____

_____

_____

_____

_____

_____

_____

_____

_____

_____

_____

_____

_____

_____

_____

_____

_____

_____

_____

_____

_____

Recall the scenes, lines in films, and passages in books and in your real-life experiences that mirrored outmoded behaviors and thoughts you've chosen to reject. Write what you remember here to serve as reminders.

_____

_____

_____

_____

_____

_____

_____

_____

_____

_____

_____

_____

_____

_____

_____

_____

_____

_____

_____

_____

_____

_____

_____

_____

_____

_____

_____

_____

List and describe the fictional people who were your heroes and heroines up until now, and write why.

_____

_____

_____

_____

_____

_____

_____

_____

_____

_____

_____

_____

_____

_____

_____

_____

_____

_____

_____

_____

_____

_____

_____

_____

_____

_____

_____

_____

List and describe the real people who were your heroes and heroines to
this point, and write why.

_____

_____

_____

_____

_____

_____

_____

_____

_____

_____

_____

_____

_____

_____

_____

_____

_____

_____

_____

_____

_____

_____

_____

_____

_____

_____

Make the Dream Real... Make it Yours

Thoughts and words are real. Both are so powerful that they promote internal and external action. As you use the words you have chosen to live with, you begin to write the script for the rest of your life.

Write to describe your reality of yourself up until now.

_____

_____

_____

_____

_____

_____

_____

_____

_____

_____

_____

_____

_____

_____

_____

_____

_____

_____

_____

_____

_____

_____

Write to describe your new reality from this moment on.

_____

_____

_____

_____

_____

_____

_____

_____

_____

_____

_____

_____

_____

_____

_____

_____

_____

_____

_____

_____

_____

_____

_____

_____

_____

_____

_____

_____

To ignite and accommodate your transformation, list the new words and conversations you will be using with your friends, family, coworkers, and fellow dreamers.

_____

_____

_____

_____

_____

_____

_____

_____

_____

_____

_____

_____

_____

_____

_____

_____

_____

_____

_____

_____

_____

_____

_____

_____

Rejoice!

By making the dream real, you make it yours. By regularly introducing new thoughts, words, and behaviors in your life, you embrace the past and leave the "unworkable" behind. The new you is growing, and you are preparing to create and live in celebration of being a dreamer of big dreams.

Living From Your Fullest Spirit Power

3

Having put the chapters on dreamwork and ridding yourself of old mindsets to practical use, we can move on to clarifying what I mean by "spirit power." What I call spirit power, you might be calling a hunch, gut feeling, sixth sense, intuition, the universal mind, the Force, God, Goddess, Source, Guardian Angel, Higher Self, Higher Power, Inner Power, or Spirit Guide. No matter what the name, what it describes is energy beyond our conscious self that works with us to recognize and accomplish our dreams. As an energizing higher self, spirit power frees each of us to tap into that part of ourselves that is increasingly expressive, dynamic, independent, and free. By using our spirit power, we begin to live in an evolving state of joy and discovery.

Start by reclaiming your childhood sense of wonderment over the simplest of things. Allow yourself to rediscover the mystery of a butterfly's flight and the curiosity accompanying the most mundane of activities. Retrain yourself to be open to all of life's possibilities for, when we listen to and heed our own inner knowing, we call our spirit power into action.

How many times have you heard stories about people who backed out of a flight because of a strange uneasiness, and the plane later crashed, or people suddenly hesitant about taking their regular route home, only to discover later that by taking an alternate road they'd avoided a serious accident? Or maybe you made a phone call to someone whose face or name kept popping into your mind and discovered that he or she was thinking about you, too. Each of those incidents is an illustration of aligning with inner knowing—that is, spirit power. What I recommend that you start doing now is to consciously and regularly tap into that power. Doing so allows you to further assume personal responsibility for your past, your present, and a rewarding future. "Tapping in," of course, requires time alone each day during which to think, feel, meditate, visualize, and write in your journal. In an environment that encourages reflective and creative thought, you can put your spirit power to work.

Claiming Your Biggest Dream

Go back and reread the new reality you described at the end Chapter 2. Are you ready to refine it—maybe even redefine it?

Let's clarify your biggest dream even further. In your journal or on your art pad, draw a number of circles. In them, write the following questions. Then write everything and anything to expand what you know and are questioning.

- ✧ *Are there any dreams hidden in my heart?*
- ✧ *What circumstances are propelling me into this new territory?*
- ✧ *What preparations will I need to make to ready myself for the realization of my biggest dream?*
- ✧ *What help will I need from other people?*
- ✧ *What help will I need from my spiritual energy?*
- ✧ *What financial resources will I need?*
- ✧ *How will I use my own personal power as I work toward my dream?*
- ✧ *What are any other concerns specific to my dream?*

Just for the fun of it, pretend that the spiritual energy available to you comes in the form of a magical work crew. There they wait, energy in action, ready to do your bidding. At your request, crew members will assist, empower, observe, facilitate, and guide you to claim your highest dream.

Without any notion of how it's going to happen, wipe your mind clear. Taking your time, allow an answer to emerge. Some people actually see the answer written on the inside of their foreheads. Others hear it, others sense it, and still others just "know" it. Even if you've never done this before, trust that your inner knowing will supply you with an answer. If not now, pay particular attention to what's being said and going on around you for the next few days. Your answer—and the answer to all your questions—may appear in a dream, in the title of a book glimpsed on a newsstand, or in a word spoken on television or on the subway. However and whenever the answers come, write them all down.

I always experience a real lightheartedness following each answer. Your sense of knowing may have you feeling it, too, or you may experience other physical or mental signs that you are gaining additional clarity about what you want, why you want it, and how you can get it. Thank those energies, and ask them to keep working.

When one of my clients tried this out she inspired herself to even greater aspiration by asking experts of the past to enter into her creative imagination times. Along with her "magical crew" she utilized the collective unconscious by asking authors, inventors, artists, politicians, spiritual leaders, and the like to enter into this designing/brainstorming/free association time. She shared that she had once asked famous architect Frank Lloyd Wright to assist her in planning her meditation room and the results were truly magical. She reports that she now realizes there is always a little magic available to her.

Transcribe your answers, whether they make sense or not, onto your art pad or into your journal. Add subcategories when related ideas come to you. Draw connecting lines showing any possible relationships. Select a colored pen that matches your enthusiasm and circle those tasks that you can joyfully embrace and accomplish by yourself. In a different energizing color, circle those tasks you will turn over to your magical work crew to manifest. An example from one of my clients is shown on page 86.

Don't limit yourself by trying to figure out how your magical work crew will accomplish their tasks. Trust their supportive energy to accomplish these tasks with perfect timing.

Having reclaimed and/or redefined your biggest dream, understand that it may take some time to assimilate what has emerged. Relax. Take several days, or weeks, to embrace what you and your magical crew are on your way to accomplishing. Take along your journal and companion workbook. When the mood strikes, record your thoughts and actions. Enjoy and celebrate the journey that you have begun.

Claiming My Biggest Dream

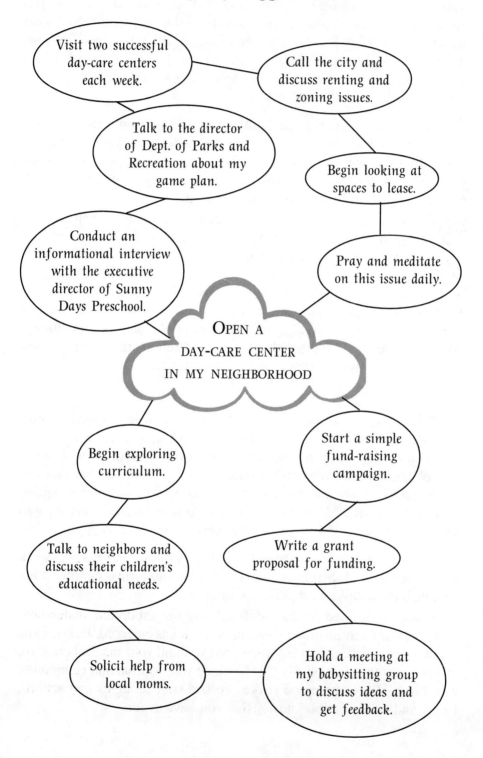

Visit two successful day-care centers each week.

Call the city and discuss renting and zoning issues.

Talk to the director of Dept. of Parks and Recreation about my game plan.

Begin looking at spaces to lease.

Conduct an informational interview with the executive director of Sunny Days Preschool.

Pray and meditate on this issue daily.

OPEN A DAY-CARE CENTER IN MY NEIGHBORHOOD

Begin exploring curriculum.

Start a simple fund-raising campaign.

Talk to neighbors and discuss their children's educational needs.

Write a grant proposal for funding.

Solicit help from local moms.

Hold a meeting at my babysitting group to discuss ideas and get feedback.

Higher Dreams, Universal Endeavors

Even if you know exactly what your dream is, there is no need to rush out and accomplish it in three weeks. Look upon this time of integration as a valuable investment of time in yourself. Use these days or weeks to think, and write, to better understand what you need and want to do to prepare yourself for this next stage in your life. Although you may continue living in the same house, same city, and/or same country, you are in a different place now. You will want to become familiar with it before venturing further.

Begin by asking yourself this question: How will the realization of my dream impact the universe?

You don't have to grasp everything before you begin, but you do need to see that your dream reaches beyond your own personal gain. Say that you want to be a world-class tennis player. Recognize that you will do more than bring thrills and inspiration to millions of like-minded hopefuls around the world. Your involvement in the industry will support tennis tournaments, sponsors, underwriters, and advertising agencies, all of which provide employment to thousands of people from executives to sign-painters and ticket-takers. Your dream enriches many!

Ask yourself: What do I need to do to prepare myself for what is to come?

Simply thinking about these things takes you to the peak of your own personal mountain for a new view of your potential. Reflection and contemplation provide space for new growth and expansion. Still, maybe you haven't extended it enough.

Read the following, and then ask yourself: How far have I extended my limits? Is my dream big or high enough, or do I need to reach even higher and dream even bigger?

In every area in which anyone has talent, expertise, and interest, there is a bigger dream waiting to be realized. The following dreamers have plans in different stages of completion, but in the acts of being conceptualized and spoken, the dreamers' dreams evolved from thinking about and recording their dreams-in-action. You may enjoy reading what some other dreamers are thinking about and claiming as they solidify their dreams. The following initial dream statements were in response to my question: "What is your biggest dream?" When you have finished reading their answers, invite your spirit power to help you release your creativity to answer that same question.

✶   A well-seasoned speechwriter in Alaska was ready to incorporate all of who she had become through the many jobs she had held. She wanted to move into an entirely new life through the realization of a new dream.

> My plan is to promote caring connection between people through international trade. My import-export business will support individual creativity and giftedness among local artists in many cultures.

✭ ✭ ✭ ✭

✶   A social worker wanted to improve the system in which she works.

> I want to practice and teach a psychosocial approach in medicine nationally to impact physicians to become more in tune with the spirit and drive of their patients, while celebrating the whole human experience.

✭ ✭ ✭ ✭

✶   A hairstylist wanted to provide more for her clients than just superior hair service. By developing her own spirituality, she could inspire them toward achieving the same deep sense of inner peace.

> My dream is to live from a state of inner peace and happiness. As I achieve this, I will become a giver of light, a shining star, using my talents to their full potential.

✭ ✭ ✭ ✭

✶   A housewife penned:

> I plan to form a network of women spanning the globe and crossing cultures. The impact will be constructive and positive, inspiring and joyful, quiet and gentle.

✭ ✭ ✭ ✭

✶   A multitalented psychologist, fearing to take a chance on herself, wrote:

> I will fully express myself as a channel for the light by being a well-paid, published author of works that combine humor, healing, and spirit.

✭ ✭ ✭ ✭

✳ Because she knows of the connection between a beautiful environ-ment and spirituality, a prominent wine consultant wants to provide a place that will allow others to tap into the power of the human spirit.

> I want to provide a Napa Valley spiritual center where world leaders in decision-making positions will come to solve problems that impact people all over the world.

★ ★ ★ ★ ★

✳ Another psychologist, reaching a point of increasing clarity, started with the following:

> I plan to bring the concepts of personal transformation into the business community. Through a thriving consulta-tion and seminar practice, travel, and a published book and series of relaxation tapes, I will bring the people-related skills learned in my clinical practice to the general work world, enabling people to communicate more effectively and expe-rience their interconnectedness both within themselves (body, mind, and spirit) and with each other.

★ ★ ★ ★ ★

✳ Arlene, a teacher from Kokomo, Indiana, who views life as wonder-ful, wants to help teens feel the same way.

> I want to build a business that gives me the opportunity to have a positive impact on a million-plus lives: a personal-image and personal-growth consulting business that helps others live their dreams. The impact will be more joy, peace, love, and happiness. People will once again whistle while they work and learn that it's okay to have a good time.

★ ★ ★ ★ ★

Other dream activators center on improving themselves. The im-portance of this cannot be overemphasized because the changes we make in ourselves have a direct positive influence on so many others. The personal investment you make in becoming whole and complete can-not help but affect those around you—and then those around them.

Eventually, all individual learning and personal growth influences the world. Just imagine what is happening right now because the fol-lowing dreams have been activated!

The following statements came from dreamers who wrote to me about claiming their dreams. Every individual's learning and personal growth influences the world. Just imagine what is happening right now because these dreams are being activated!

I want to celebrate being at peace within myself, to be a non-anxious presence to others, and to encourage and empower others to find and live from that deep place of peace, too. I am the wife of a corporate executive and the mother of two adult sons. As I pursued my own career as artist, writer, and teacher, I found being superwoman increasingly debilitating. Burnt out and suffering from depression, I moved from being driven by outer dictates to living from a deeper spiritual level. As I trust my creative spirit, I am able to be more open, honest, and authentic with myself and others and as I care for myself, I am able to be a healing presence to others. My life is now a comfortable balance between being and doing. As the old song says, "Let there be peace on earth, and let it begin with me!"

⋆ ⋆ ⋆ ⋆ ⋆

I will realize my biggest dream by releasing my authentic self and going forward alone on a new journey of personal growth and new experiences.

⋆ ⋆ ⋆ ⋆ ⋆

Being a part of a community of people who truly work together for the good of the group and always strive to help others, that is my biggest dream.

⋆ ⋆ ⋆ ⋆ ⋆

My biggest dream is to write a novel and have it published.

⋆ ⋆ ⋆ ⋆ ⋆

My biggest dream is to be fabulously abundant, by empowering myself and others to live their dream. When each person is living his or her dream, the world will be a place where everyone will be living a blessed life.

⋆ ⋆ ⋆ ⋆ ⋆

My biggest dream is to develop a system that will help people find their way.

★ ★ ★ ★

I want to tell stories that whisper their secrets to me. These stories have lives of their own, and are meant to be passed down generation through generation for the education and upliftment of all mankind.

★ ★ ★ ★

I want to use my God-given talent in the art field to help myself, my family, and others and to prepare for retirement. Each person with whom I share my art will hopefully receive joy and pass it on to others. Each person with whom I instruct my talents/ skills will hopefully use information learned to better his or her life and will share with others, and the cycle continues.

★ ★ ★ ★

By writing and directing a movie I will somehow help women to understand how astonishing powerful they are.

★ ★ ★ ★

My biggest dream is to spread my happiness.

★ ★ ★ ★

The universe calls each of us to be the very best we can be, to give the best of ourselves, and to inspire others to help us use our power to attain our highest dreams. The following statement took me out of the ordinary and served as a reminder that this is where I want to live all of the time. Getting in touch with the largeness of oneself is mystical, marvelous, magnificent, and mysterious, too!

Unfortunately, not everyone lives in a world that's mystical, marvelous, magnificent, and mysterious—or feels much hope of doing so! The following is a classic illustration of the broken spirits of individuals, and nations, as well.

While traveling through Yugoslavia in the summer of 1990, I met an engineer whose skills were no longer in demand during his nation's turmoil, so he took a job as a tour guide. In this way, he could make some money while sharing with others the country he loves. I asked him why he felt his nation was in such serious trouble. "The trouble with my country is," he said, "that the people have given up their dreams." As you can guess, his answer disturbed and inspired me. This is still true in many areas of the world today—and compelling evidence exists to support his conclusions.

Now, more than ever, each of us must believe in our own individual importance within the grand scheme of things—even if we cannot visualize that scheme in its entirety. Don't compromise; believe in yourself, and make the changes necessary to have all your dreams come true!

Improving our own condition will empower and inspire those around us. I don't want to make this sound easy or without risk or setbacks. What I do want to say is that, despite sensible reasons for doubt, and maybe even despair, you must retain a passionate optimism while you face your realities. Consciously looking on the bright side allows us to select what is possible instead of giving in to hopelessness and helplessness. What we knew as children is true: We knew what we wanted and often expected to be supported to realize our wishes, hopes, and dreams. We may have given that control to others for a time, but—as adults—we need not continue doing so. For that very reason, I encourage you to make an effort to associate with people whose futuristic ideas you admire.

Make it a point to surround yourself with practical and creative idealists, because together each of us is more than we are alone. Together, we share ideas and fine-tune them, exposing one another to the process of working toward the highest good of all. Those people I have come to admire most are those who recognize that it is not only futile, but globally self-destructive, to continue resuscitating 20th-century institutions and procedures. In the coming years we must explore new ways of viewing and doing everything. For instance, after an earthquake in Los Angeles, California, I personally witnessed an interesting transformation. Because employees couldn't get to work, companies allowed those with home computers to work at home. Not only had employers found a new way of working through a crisis, but working at home proved to be more effective for many workers than coming into the office! How many acts of nature or Earth-shaking events do we need before we begin improving outmoded systems?

By listening, observing, and researching with other progressive thinkers in science, social services, politics, business, government, and the arts, we can all learn new ways to replace obsolete practices and to use innovative procedures to revitalize tired infrastructures. From this will emerge a more enlightened world in which individuals increasingly assume total responsibility for themselves and their own dreams. New dreams and other inventions, methods, ideas, and approaches are always needed, too—maybe yours! Are you regularly setting aside quality time each day to align with your biggest dream—to think about it, visualize it, plan it, and prepare to live it?

Unleashing Your Mental Energy

There is immense energy released simply by imagining an empowered populace. Envisioned, those people who are intent upon nurturing responsible self-fulfillment can replace a society bogged down in meting out punishment to miscreants. Picture a world where governments sponsor machines of peace instead of war. Visualize the rebuilding of our aging roads and bridges generating as many jobs as it takes to produce increasingly arcane methods of nuclear mayhem.

Most of us want to live in balance, peace, and harmony. Few want gangs to represent a threat to each other or the rest of us. We don't want there to be a need for more jails for juveniles or adults. What personal action can you take to bring more peace and harmony to yourself, to your home, to your community, and to your workplace that will effect change in the way things are now? If you are a parent, what can you do to give positive direction to kids in your neighborhood? How effective are after-school activities in your community? If you are a businessperson, what can you do to improve your work environment? First, find out what is already available and provided. How can it be improved? What action can you take to help, support, or empower? What if schools and colleges taught self-awareness and higher consciousness to everyone involved in after-school programs and organizations? They, in turn, could teach caregivers to teach children to fulfill themselves in a healthy and peaceful way. With consciously aware people teaching others how to fulfill themselves, everybody wins! Just imagine: less crime, less homelessness, fewer throw-away children, and more people capable of caring about others because they've learned appropriate ways to communicate and love themselves.

So there is much to do, dream activator. After the age of 3, many learned to protect or hide our creative and spirit energies. Are you still guarding yours because of old fears that surround revealing your inner self? Or are you afraid that someone will steal your ideas? Do you fear that being more than you appear would threaten your job? Cost you friends? Hurt your family? To unleash and use spiritual and mental energies, you must begin to move beyond doubt and fear. By choosing to do something positive with your past experiences, you move to a higher place— and by doing so, you lift your part of the universe. Let me illustrate this by telling another story about myself.

Accepting Personal Power

Some years ago I was at a school-board meeting where it became clear that my opinions were not wanted. It was a new experience: I'd been a master teacher for years, developed innovative classroom procedures, trained many student teachers for K–6 classrooms and co-created a K–6 school-within-a-school. Now, elected non-educators didn't want to hear what I had to say. Suddenly, I knew what it felt like to be powerless—and I didn't like it. Who among us wants to be where we are not valued—where what we must do is diametrically opposed to our inner knowing, instincts, and training? That became the first of many uncomfortable meetings.

For weeks, I struggled with my feelings of hurt, dismissal, confusion, and fear—the usual steps in the decision-making process. You see, I loved everything about teaching: the kids, the smell of chalk, the personal and professional chatter in the teacher's room. I had a very strong sense that was time for me to move on and to choose a new path. What I needed, I decided, was to take a leave of absence and pursue my dream of designing and creating a private school project and also go back to college for an additional degree in psychology. This would allow me to upgrade my educational experiences and skills for use with a broader audience and prepare for a counseling profession. (Although it took only the last few sentences to explain my decision process, please don't think that it came easily. Changing even one part of my life seriously impacted my relationship with my husband and our four children. It also significantly challenged our family income and health-insurance coverage.) I was just fine—until the day I packed up my teaching supplies and closed the door at The New Age School for the last time. Then I went through what I call the "crazies"—which is nothing but unreasoning fear. *What am I doing?* I asked myself. *Leaving a well-paying job that I adore?* Even though I knew that the new place I was heading would bring me even more joy, what was it going to take to get there? Fortunately, my fear was only momentary, because fear is simply a lack of clarity or focus. I knew where I was going; I knew what my biggest dream was.

Even with clarity, however, it was not easy to take a new path. Yet I made it, and that is because, from the moment I realized that I had outgrown my former profession, I also understood that my response to the changing focus in education was just the nudge I needed to move on. Understanding the process allowed me to activate myself, which put me back to go into my own power. Knowing this made studying, doing the schoolwork, and interning for thousands of hours a rewarding experience. From there, I went on to establish a personal-growth coaching/consulting business, to design and facilitate innovative work-shops, and then to author and have published three books and related workbooks. That is what I dream and want for you: to be able to recognize what it is that drains your personal and spirit energy; to move beyond it; to experience the thrill of going within to reacquaint yourself with the source of those powers; to receive inner direction; to feel the exhilaration that comes from discovering, and working toward your biggest dreams, and the satisfaction of having done so.

Altering Outmoded Concepts of Power

Our understanding of power comes not only from observation, but also from listening to the stories and directions of earlier generations. Many people don't go for their really big dreams because they don't want to be perceived as selfish or self-centered. That's why they turn their personal power over to family members, friends, or employers. Others, frequently those who were physically, verbally, and/or emotionally abused as children, grow up determined to do unto others as was done unto them. These are the power-grabbers who must be "king of the mountain" and who consistently keep everyone else below them to maintain a position at the top. Although different, both misuses of power limit an individual's ability to move ahead into living a life of contribution.

Are you holding yourself back because you fear your own powers? A client once confessed, "My God, if I let go of all the power that's in me, I'd blow everyone else off the planet!" Truly believing that, she deliberately kept from going forth with her deepest held dream. Instead, she devoted her superior organizational skills and intelligence to community projects. This is not to suggest that community projects are unsuitable as biggest dreams; they just weren't hers!

The power feared by my client, the queen of community projects, was the result of her childhood programming. "Don't be smarter than the boys," her mother warned. "You'll never get anything that way!" Note that mother said "anything," not "anywhere," because a large percentage of women of her generation had gone nowhere except into marriage. Only poor women had jobs. Few middle- and upper-class women were educated to become professionals. Fewer still were those women who were nationally and internationally known and respected. Congresswoman Millicent Fenwick of New Jersey, who served from the 1930s to the late 1980s as an author, congresswoman, ambassador, and U.S. advisor on civil rights, was a rare exception. Many women concentrated on getting "things" from their male providers. My client continued to carry her 1940s–1950s fear of being so aggressive that she might offend men and be ostracized by other women, even though she encouraged her daughters to tackle the professional male world. She remains a victim of fears instilled in her when she was a teenager. Those fears must be examined, and then dissipated, if she is ever to use her power appropriately and fully. I frequently remind, and encourage, her to dream big!

Assuming Total Responsibility

Most people carry their fear of one or more of their childhood authority figures into adulthood. How do we acknowledge their influence and power over us? At one extreme, by imitating them; at the other, by consciously behaving contrary to their behavior. Both are examples of abandoning powers that are rightfully ours to an old belief system. Unfortunately, it's like an old, familiar dance—with each partner knowing the steps so well he or she doesn't even question them or consider it is time to create a new dance.

Margi had a dominating father who dismissed her every opinion as "silly." By the age of 16, she had learned that, if she wanted her father to like her, she would have to keep her ideas to herself. Now, at 30, she has had a series of romances that died when she was unable to tell her suitors what she wanted from their relationship. Even now, many men and women are terrified that people won't like them if they assert even a little power. Although Margi's father had no conscious plan to turn his teenager into an uncommunicative adult, that is what he did. That he continues to disagree with everything she says is, in a perverse way, his attempt to keep her dependent upon his approval. What he doesn't realize is that she despises herself for not having the courage to talk back to him. Before she can get on with her life, she must demand that he allow her opinions to be voiced. Then she must start relationships off by letting the other person know what she likes, dislikes, and expects. Doing this firmly, but in a non-threatening way, Margi has now realized this will take time and work. By taking action she is activating her own personal and spiritual powers.

The unwillingness to assume these powers definitely is not limited to women. A man came to one of my workshops who he shared that he had wanted his wife to accompany him, but that she had "too much to do" to participate. It was as if her need to keep a spotless house and dinner on the table at 5 p.m. was more important than anything that he wanted to do. At lunchtime I gave the group an assignment to get in touch with paying attention to every moment and then to record what was going on. The man lived close by so went home for lunch and, because he had enjoyed the morning, asked his wife to come back with him. "It would be fun for both of us to be tapping into this experience," he reported himself as saying. Her response was, "Well, I can't. I have to fix a casserole for dinner!"

Was she letting him know that fixing a meal is more important than going with him? What he said upon returning was, "So I came back alone, because I suddenly remembered how many times she has used this type of excuse not to do things." Later he wrote and shared that he finally understood that her unwillingness to join him was more than a rejection of a single event they might have enjoyed together: It was her unwillingness to join him in revitalizing their final years together.

In my "Write Your Life" workshops I encourage people that it is fun, exciting, and satisfying to record your life and to learn from *all* life experiences. Although there is power in revisiting a memory, it is vital to remember that what you cannot change is also part of your story. It is a temptation, when reviewing our lives, to get caught up in reexperiencing events where we failed, or were used, or even abused. But the world has—and we have—changed. In earlier years, we might not have been as secure or confident as we are now. So now we would not deal with that situation in the same way. It is essential to examine but not to reactivate old feelings of powerlessness and anger. Instead, when we look back, it is important to note the progress in ourselves in dealing with potentially dangerous or harmful situations. In this way, we do not relinquish the confidence we have developed over the years by meeting and mastering many of life's challenges.

As I presented this information to another audience, a woman in her 60s listened to me with growing alarm. As I explained that it was also necessary to go back and reacquaint ourselves with earlier dreams we either manifested or forgot, she became quite agitated. Tentatively, she raised her hand. Was I saying, she wanted to know, that she should take a closer look at what she had wanted before she was raising children, taking care of her husband, and doing her volunteer work? Yes, I replied—and to recall all the dreams she'd had while caring for a family and doing volunteer work.

"I was too busy to dream," she said, then, after a pause, she asked, "Are you saying that I could make a different life for myself now?"

"As you start looking back over your life," I enthusiastically responded, "you will automatically become more active in planning what kind of life you want in the future. That's because when we evaluate what happened to earlier dreams, we become more conscious of how seldom we really designed the life we are living right now. And looking back is one of the steps toward experiencing joy in living a life that we have consciously designed."

"That's what you're talking about?" she demanded. "Joy? You mean being joyful all the time—every day?"

"What a wonderful question," I laughed. Then, going to the right side of the board, I wrote the word *joy*. Walking across the room to the left side of the board, I drew an arrow running all the way to *joy*. Above the sheath of the arrow, I wrote the words *happiness, sadness, pain, loss, fun, depression, fear, betrayal, disappointment, anger, powerlessness, discomfort, confusion,* and *celebration*.

"These," I said, "are the human experiences each of us goes through to get to the state of living in joy. Please notice that the arrow goes through all those life experiences before it reaches the target." So, if you are suffering from any negative experience, know that on the other side of it is joy. As children often illustrate, joy in living is our natural state. Only as we progress into adolescence and adulthood do we learn to deny that. And those who do not allow themselves to progress through pain, loss, abuse, an addiction, or death of a loved one will linger forever in recovery. People clinging to, or remaining in, the recovery process often experience little joy because they deny their own personal power and spiritual energy to move on into living and celebrating their realized dreams.

During that same workshop, a man sitting in the front row began a playful heckling when I urged people to examine their lives. "So," he asked, "what do *you* do when a family member has a problem? Ignore him to pursue your own interests?"

"Encourage and direct him to an expert where he can get help," I replied.

"What do you do when friends call and interrupt you?" he pursued.

"I got an answering machine, so I could ask them to call back at a convenient time for me," I replied. It was the beginning of a daylong set of challenges and tests. He wasn't rude, or even unkind. In fact, he was a charming man who loved to question me to answer and to clarify my ideas. I enjoyed listening to his theories as well. However, at the end of the day, he asked, half-laughingly, "Do you have any friends?" It broke him up when I replied, "No!" Then everyone laughed. I followed up by saying that among thousands of acquaintances, I have a great many people who consider me their friend. I treasure my friends who are honest, courageous, and true to themselves and their dreams. Many people worry about offending others with the strength of their beliefs. How easily they will dilute their own powers whenever they find their opinions threatening others. Diluting any of your power keeps you from following your dreams. Although some people deny their personal powers, others wield it, with unhappy consequences for themselves and others.

Eric, a young client of mine bucked family expectation by not attending college. *Why go?* he reasoned. His family had invested heavily in art and antiques and was about to open a gallery. Since he had grown up listening to his parents and grandparents discussing their growing collections, he figured he knew as much—if not more—than most people on the subject. The family gallery opened when Eric was in his early 20s, and, because he was energetic and knowledgeable, they allowed him to assume the position of executive director. Although Eric knows antiques, art, and artists, he didn't know how to appropriately manage the responsibility the family has given him. That's partially because position and its inherent power were given to him rather than earned. He has had no training in motivating others, setting a good example, or restraining a natural sense of leadership that appears to be arrogance.

It is rare that desire alone is enough when a business (a gallery, in this case) relies upon the reciprocity of professors and experts holding graduate degrees. It may be necessary for those in charge to have equivalent training and expertise. Eric's enthusiasm may be adequate, but it will be to his advantage to obtain additional training in order to make the gallery a success.

Understanding the Danger That Comes From Ego

The difference between the power of spirit energy and the power of ego is enormous. If you find that using your power is more tiring than inspiring, there is probably still some part of you that wants power for power's sake alone. If you are battling each step of the way to motivate those around you to get things done, reevaluate not only the group goals, but your own. If you feel a need to always be on the alert, to eliminate or squelch someone who might be better equipped, understand that it is ego—not his or her qualifications or ambition—that is sapping your power. And if, even in moments of financial, social, political, or bureaucratic victory, you feel obliged to dominate and manipulate those around you, it is your insecurity at work. Know that the power you are now wielding is condemning you to a life of mediocrity, and even that will not last forever. Soon someone else will be king or queen of your lonely hill. For those of you who are dominated by someone who is working from ego, trust your own source of power. If the person chooses not to change, get away! You cannot allow this type of power to squash yours. Remember the words of Albert Einstein: "Great spirits have always encountered violent opposition from mediocre minds."

One way to determine whether you are empowering or being driven by ego is to ask yourself: *Do I usually inspire and energize those around me?*

Learning to Respond Without Ego

Energizing and empowering others come from ego-less responses that honor the other person's feelings. Ego-less responses, especially questions, can often illustrate respect for what the other person knows. By honoring and respecting that, the respondent removes potential resistance and avoids hurting feelings.

Check your automatic responses with those given in the following situations:

A child comes home from school full of enthusiasm for what he has learned. "Did you know that it's a myth that George Washington chopped down a cherry tree?" he asks his mother. Ego-less response: "If I knew that, I'd forgotten. Every day you surprise me with how much you learn!"

★ ★ ★ ★

With their son's ball game over, a family is in the car heading home. Although his son's team won, Dad can see many ways the kids can improve. However, until an adult tells them that they need to be better at what they are doing, most kids are pretty much pleased just to have participated. Trouble starts when parents try to point out how the team could improve. Children in sports already have coaches who are there to teach and guide; what they need from their parents is support! Ego-less question to the son: "How do you feel about the game?" Whatever the youngster's statement, the ego-less response would be to listen and say something such as, "It's a real pleasure for me to watch you and your friends play!"

★ ★ ★ ★

Married less than a year, newlyweds are at odds over an unscheduled purchase made by one or the other. "Did we really need that?" the non-buyer asks. Ego-less response of buyer: "Why do you ask?" Ego-less response of non-buyer: "Because we have only so much money, and I want us to have a firm financial base." If the couple has similar values and both are cognizant of watching spending to reach their common goals, these responses provide an opportunity to discuss earlier agreements. New purchases can then be negotiated and planned for, not fought over.

★ ★ ★ ★ ★

Outraged that a state politician voted against a gun control measure, a woman wrote a letter accusing him of selling out to gun interests. Upon receiving it, he immediately called her to explain precisely how the proposed legislation was flawed. "Why didn't you fix those flaws when the proposition was being written?" she demanded. "Because I'm concentrating my energy on prevention," he replied. "I'm writing legislation for young children." He went on to suggest that she help him put on a public forum about gun control. Her ego-less response put direct responsibility onto him—and herself: "A public forum is for those who don't know," she said. "You and I know precisely what needs to be done. So, I don't expect you to write gun control legislation, but I expect you to keep abreast of that which is written by others, note your suggested additions or deletions, and then send it to me. I'll spend the time it takes to let politicians and the public know what's going on!"

★ ★ ★ ★ ★

A recovering substance abuser demands of a close friend, "Prove to me that my life will be better without drugs." Ego-less response: "You tell me: How much better would your life be without drugs?" "Well, I wouldn't have to worry about the police, or overdosing, or running out of money." Ego-less response: "So, with all that energy, money, and time, what's your biggest dream?" By not passing judgment in the very beginning, the friend not only keeps the substance abuser accountable, he encourages him to dream and plan ahead for a happier, drug-free future.

★ ★ ★ ★ ★

A woman with an aging parent complains to a friend, "My 86-year-old mother is driving me crazy with her negativity and constant demands. I just don't know what to do." Ego-less response: "How do you want to be treated when you're 86?" Whether the mother has always been negative and demanding, or just recently became so, this response shifts the daughter's complaints into another dimension. Suddenly, she can see things from an older person's point of view. Then she can decide how to proceed for the good of all concerned.

★ ★ ★ ★ ★

Dream activators always try to respond in honest, creative, loving, intuitive, joyful, expressive, effective, and responsible ways. In this way they become more sure of themselves, direct, dynamic, energetic, and free. Choose to be, or work towards becoming, a dream activator operating from spirit energy and personal power! Take time to reevaluate your new habits, and record your new thinking in the workbook and your journal.

Recognizing Ego in Yourself

If you feel that people feel unsafe around you, that you are beset by incompetent employees or coworkers against whom you must protect yourself with secrecy, anger, or fear, know this: Before you can achieve—and live peacefully with—your biggest dream, you must learn to redirect and rid yourself of that kind of ego-driven power seeking. In fact, noticing it to make getting rid of it is your next dream step.

Begin by asking yourself: What are my concerns, and my fears, about igniting my spirit power and celebrating being powerful? *Write in your journal, or draw pictures of yourself on your art pad, of a time that you felt these concerns and fears.*

Remember that to rid ourselves of fears and insecurities, we need to avoid controlling or subduing others for personal gain. Any time that your life's work requires you to ignore others' needs and feelings, you are in danger of subduing them to meet your own needs. Spiritual power, you see, comes in whenever we are empowering others and ourselves.

Denying Personal Power

What if, instead of being ego-ridden, you are a person who denies or negates your power? Many people distract themselves from assuming responsibility for themselves by keeping busy with gossip, travel, meetings, or working too much. Others consciously hand over their power to friends, family members, partners, spouses, teachers, attorneys, politicians, doctors, drugs and alcohol, business leaders, and bosses. However, although some people escape their responsibility to and for themselves, millions of others are taking their power back, renewing their spirit, demanding accountability of those who serve us, and examining alternatives to long-held practices. By activating their spirit power, ordinary people are transforming their own lives, and taking an active part in changing government, medicine, the law, education, recovery programs, industry, and businesses. It's time to take another look at power: how you claim it, how you express it, and how you use it in your world and the world.

Ego and Power: The Volatile Two

Are you using your personal power to be in control or in charge? The need to be in control is always about control *over,* rather than sharing power *with*. Rikki, a San Diego, California, county employee for many years had been assuming more and more of the daily responsibilities that her boss was ignoring. Not only was she irritated at having the extra work, but she was angry that he took credit for how well she was doing it. Together we identified the problem here was: her ego! The following exercise allowed her to identify where the problem lay, which allowed her to move beyond the barrier of ego and start working seriously on her dream.

Using Rikki's situation as an example, substitute one of your own issues and answer the same questions.

☆ What's troubling you?
(Rikki's answer: "I'm doing twice the work for half the money.")

☆ What do you want?
(Rikki: "To prove the boss is taking advantage of me.")

☆ Why?
(Rikki: "To receive acknowledgement for all the work I've done!")

☆ Will that bring you satisfaction?
(Rikki thinks awhile before responding: "No. I want him to do his own work, too.")

☆ Let's take this higher: What do you want for the highest good of both you and your boss?
(Rikki: "For us each to do our own work.")

☆ So what do you need to do?
(Rikki: "I need to stop doing his work.")

☆ Are you going to do that immediately?
(Rikki: "Well, I'm paying you for this advice, so I'd better get on with it right away!" (And she did!))

Can you get on with changing your attitude about power?

Having gotten rid of negative thought through positive action, Rikki freed herself to unleash her creative energy. What was equally important is that she realized the ego battle going on with her boss, who, by not doing his own work, was contributing to a work environment that was stifling for her. When Rikki stopped, so did his energy-sapping negative pattern. Now, instead of wasting energy being angry at being used, Rikki is taking charge by changing, growing, and planning her future.

Writing a New Definition

It's time to move beyond our old operating procedures. First, you must decide that giving them up is what you want to do. Next, clarify what self-established rules you want to live by. The fact is if you have a great deal invested in living in poor health, you might not want to become well and whole. If you are more comfortable in just getting by each month than in living with the concept of affluence, you may never have enough money! How many people do you know or have you read about who don't align or celebrate life even though they have healthy bank accounts? By accepting that poverty or lack of security is your destiny, you may feel poor even if you win a million dollars! The same goes for those who think they aren't smart enough or pretty enough or that they are victims, or who see themselves as always in recovery. If that is what you choose to believe, that's what you'll be. If you want to be free of your old concepts, move beyond where you are. Choose to move beyond whatever has hindered you to experience wholeness. It is your choice! The following examples of individuals who rose above protecting their ego and personal limitations to change the lives of their countrymen and women may inspire you.

In India, Mahatma Ghandi envisioned what would be right for his country and was willing to die for it. Although he chose to oppose the ruling English government in nonviolent ways, his actions placed him in danger every day. But by living what he believed, he moved millions of Indians into a new understanding of their own personal and collective consciousness. And he influenced foreign attitudes toward his countrymen as well. Ghandi's actions inspired others to use nonviolent ways to change their societies.

Martin Luther King, Jr. awakened a new awareness to serious social injustice in America. John Fitzgerald Kennedy lit the spark of overwhelming powerful public response by introducing the concept of a Peace Corps. No one in Washington was adequately prepared for the demand that followed, but the challenges were met and a dream was realized. That's what happens when a dreamer empowers others by sharing his or her vision for the future. History records that the people who did this initiated lasting change in whichever century they lived. *But these are well-known and famous people,* you say, *what about me?* Common people who saw a need and met it have also made history. You and your ideas are just as valuable as any great dreamers in history!

When retired librarian Maggie Kuhn grew angry over the plight of poor elderly Americans, her objections started a movement that evolved into the Gray Panthers, a group of over-60 activists who lobbied for new laws and rules governing the rights of older people. When she was in her mid-20s and an unknown reporter, Gloria Steinem objected to the misperceptions then damaging women by exposing the chauvinist mindset in a series of scathing articles. She opened the door to a new level of understanding and awareness. Steinem remains a visible champion of human dignity. Living congruently with the belief that true power is energized by love and concern for others, as well as ourselves, allows us to use the power of our own spirit and often realize a dream.

Yet, how many people do you know who are willing to stand up and say, *I am powerful, and I take full responsibility for being all of who I can be!* Much of our unwillingness to do that comes from our earlier programming. As teenagers, many are encouraged to be modest—to at least appear to subdue or even apologize for personal power. Captains of sports teams, for instance, traditionally verbalize or show with body language an "aw shucks, it was nothing" attitude toward their accomplishments during awards ceremonies. I'm not encouraging arrogance, but there is nothing wrong with admitting that you've worked very hard to be successful—and that you are pleased and proud that your commitment and hard work paid off. We do the same thing when we encourage our children, friends, family members, and coworkers to downplay their intelligence or abilities. It's better, the general public says, for them to exhibit good looks, trendy clothes, and popularity. By promoting false modesty and empty-headedness, we strip many of their heartfelt dreams or their personal power. The results can be seen all around us: men and women who measure themselves by celebrities or beautiful models who tell them what brands, fashions, and cars they need to buy to be considered successful or acceptable.

We must make a conscious effort to reinstate our natural powers of the spirit and individuality. When you accept the naturalness of this combination and use it to accomplish a dream, exuberance replaces boredom and complacency. Power of the spirit flourishes in those of us who are so secure in what we know to be our destiny that we don't need to depend upon anyone else's applause or compliance.

Using the power of your spirit is like having access to the ultimate library. When I said this in a Live Your Dream workshop, one person asked, "How do I get a card?" "What a great question!" I replied. The answer is by clearing away all the obstacles and fully accepting your power so that you can access the power of everything around you. That it has been there all along is not the point. It's like not using the public library that is so conveniently nearby. Suddenly, a road ignored beckons us. There is, for instance, so much information available to everyone on the Internet. Are you taking advantage of that unlimited resource yet? No, you say, because it is still in theoretical form, and therefore unavailable. Ah-ha— not true! If access to this highway has moved from the unconscious to the conscious mind, then it's real. So, getting your library card requires nothing but investigation, perseverance, and commitment. Then, the minute information comes online, you are ready, and thereby gaining immediate access to all the communicable intelligence you will ever need. But that access is possible only when you make yourself ready for, and then activate, your own abilities—or your own power. Otherwise if unused, you'll be lingering at signs that say *caution, expect delays, detours,* or *dead end.*

Combining Spiritual Power and Personal Power

It is exciting to see dreamers becoming dream activators simply by putting spirit and personal powers into action. Spirit and personal powers differ in that spirit power is the force that is innately ours; we are born with spirit energy. Personal power is often based upon what you know, what you learn—in some cases, where you learned it—and who you know. Personal power is the authority that you consciously assume for yourself and is at times given to you by others. Combining the two leads to celebrations as you travel towards your biggest dream.

Visible Signs of Spirit and Personal Power

To remind myself that even the expression and use of my power need to take a lighthearted turn now and then, I do not hold back when, on a golden day in fall, I feel the urge to twirl, childlike, in a pile of brightly colored leaves. I don't care that onlookers might not approve. There I whirl, arms outstretched in the sunlight, laughing. By illustrating my love of being alive, I encourage others to cast aside their inhibitions in ways of their own. Some might want to illustrate their own passion for being alive by laughing along—or joining me. And later on when each of us remembers that golden day, we each smile, remembering the joy of being uninhibited in the love of a beautiful day. Shedding our inhibitions makes us surer of ourselves, more resilient, more determined than ever to be true to ourselves. That alone makes us more powerful, and when we align our power with our spirit energy, we can fulfill our destiny. The following people have evolved from wishing to dream activators by tapping into their spirit energy. These are the words they use to describe it:

Accepting the power and energy of my spirit means getting out of my own physical presence and living in my God presence, where all my power lives.

★ ★ ★ ★ ★

To listen within. To pay attention. To act on the guidance given. And to trust that if I am in harmony within, all of life around me is also doing its "right dance" as well.

★ ★ ★ ★ ★

Stepping into my spirit is like having wings on my shoes. I am lifted and carried forward, almost as if I were a dandelion seed, finding a new home where this fair wind blows.

★ ★ ★ ★ ★

Clearing my present circumstances and finding harmony without too many attachments to the outcome of things!

★ ★ ★ ★ ★

By welcoming my power, I know myself better each day. This means knowing with clarity and confidence what needs to be done. It allows me to know me.

★ ★ ★ ★ ★

Stepping into my power means not being ashamed or scared to be, beautiful, shining, alone, together, too overwhelming, too shy, too sexy, too late, too flighty, too attached. It means accepting myself no matter what and forgiving myself all the time in different ways, by seeing perspective that one moment leads to the next in a natural organic way. It means trusting that this is the way it was meant to be and life has a natural rhythm, beauty, and grace. It means trusting the universe and my place in it. It also means not fearing life or death equally.

Embracing my own powers means realizing myself for who I truly am, not as others perceive me to be.

Stepping into my power means I am letting my heart lead the way.

Stepping into my power means I can write anytime I want to write.

I am truly living and celebrating myself, my life, my dreams, when I step into my power!

How Much Power Do You Want?

How much do you need? How much will be required—all the time, some of the time, or rarely? What choices does the realization of your dream involve? How will you use your power of the spirit to achieve it? How is it different from achieving it through the power of the ego?

Because self-examination is a necessary first step, write to revisit and refresh your answers to the important who, what, where, when, and why questions:

✧ *Why am I here?*

✧ *What do I want out of life?*

✧ *What do I want to accomplish or contribute?*

✧ *Where do I belong?*

✧ *Where do I want to go?*

✧ *When should I make my move?*

And is it your power you want to use, or someone else's? All too often, we borrow other people's power, even when there is no longer a need to do so. How many married women continue to ask their husband's permission to go out with female friends long after getting used to socializing without him? How many men are reluctant to make business-related social plans without first consulting with their wives? Is their hesitancy politeness? Consideration? Or a symbol that the relationship would have evolved faster and more had old habits been abandoned? Do we cheat our partners of their growth when we treat them at 50 as we did at 26? Is not allowing our relationships and dreams to grow a major cause of separation or divorce?

A retired major-league baseball player made some interesting remarks during a television interview. When asked about his personal life, he stated that it was no wonder that his earlier marriages had failed. What he had come to realize since retiring, he said, was that management deliberately fostered adolescent behavior in professional ball players. Provided with every material object a person could ever want, public adoration, and outrageous salaries, players had no reason to grow beyond what they had been when first drafted. When did he realize that he was being denied that growth during his career? Not until much later, he said.

Had he believed at the time that he possessed, and used, personal power during those years? Certainly. But, even while he was demanding—and getting—enormous amounts of money, owners and managers had the real power: what he had was the big bat, or the fastball, or the legs. Do you know when you are being stifled, or manipulated, by bosses, agents, partners, family members, and friends?

If you aren't learning something new and taking the steps to realize your dreams, you are easy prey for those who would rob you of your powers. Professional sports heroes are prime examples, because they have been led to believe that acquiring a huge amount of money is the answer to their fulfillment. Too many have discovered that it is the answer to only one dream, one that may end all too soon. No matter how outstanding his or her talent or skill, everyone needs to keep expanding and exploring the mind. For high school and college athletes that means attending classes and committing themselves to learning academic subjects—even when coaches and teachers would make special allowances or let them off the hook. For those professional athletes who have not continued their schooling, it means doing so in the off season. For every young adult in the world, it means making learning a habit. For every adult, no matter the age, it means becoming a fully functioning human being by being curious about what you don't know. Learn! Will living true to yourself and your wishes, hopes, and dreams require changing or leaving friends, coworkers, and maybe even family members behind?

Sometimes, but again, as you have already discovered, it's amazing how those around you change when you do. Although I would hope that partners would grow together, it is not always possible. In the same way we may outgrow organizations, programs, and careers that no longer inspire or serve us. To be true to ourselves, we must go forward and beyond. So how much power does a person want or need? As much as it takes to survive even what appears to be absolute powerlessness. Some former prisoners of war tell of being stripped of everything: nourishing food, personal belongings, clothes, companionship, and light. Some took what seemed to be the easy way and gave up; they turned their bodies and minds over to their jailers and let them do whatever they wished. One prisoner outwitted his captors by tapping into his own resources: He began planning in intricate detail the house he would build upon release. Day by day throughout his torturous imprisonment, he drew mental pictures of walls, flooring, joists, wiring, and plumbing. By using creative and spiritual powers to survive, he made his imaginary house real. And real it is! After being released, that house was built identically to the plans he'd imagined. Tapping into the power of the spirit is the result of embracing and accepting one's personal powers.

When I first asked myself what accepting all of my spiritual energy and personal power meant to me, I had to start with what was real. And what is real for me are the voices in my head. Sound crazy? Well, the voices I hear, and the insights they give, are very real to me! Those voices correspond with the reality of an idea as opposed to an achieved dream. To illustrate: Does a building project become a reality when it is conceived, when it is committed to a drawing board, when the wood is purchased, when it is built, or when it is painted or varnished? To me, an idea is real the instant it takes shape in the dreamer's mind—just as a book is real, or a painting is real, the moment it is conceived in the author's or artist's mind. Taking the time to have the clarity of mind to create it is often the hard part; implementing it takes attention, commitment, desire, and action!

A building project is, of course, a measurable reality. Curiosity is also real, although it cannot be weighed or measured. Television is real, even though most of us do not know the full process of it getting from the studio into our living room. Although television is real, how about virtual reality? Space travel is real, but quantum leaps are still beyond us. In your lifetime alone, how many things that you take for granted have gone from theory to reality? What's next? And when do those new ideas become realities?

During the process of deciding to leave the teaching profession, I had to ask myself some pretty basic questions. *Why am I on this planet at this time in history? What was I willing to do to find out?* That is when I had to believe in myself enough to step into the "void." That doesn't mean that I literally stepped off a cliff, although stepping into the unknown seemed like it at the time. Whether it was a move made from desperation, or faith, it came from my need to move beyond all that was keeping me from serving a larger humanity and making more of a contribution. Wasn't I doing that when I directed in my innovative classrooms? At that moment, yes. But the handwriting was on the wall for the local school board was moving away from what I believed to be best for children. Being a futurist, I wanted to prepare children for the new millennium, not take a step backward. Because I could not live congruently with what was expected, it was necessary for me to move on. This meant creating a new reality for myself. It required me to tap into my personal power, and then activate it, for a whole new challenge. How much spirit and personal power do you need to accomplish your dream? As much as you need to make the move to pursue a dream and bring it into reality! How do you combine them? By diminishing your need to force others to do your bidding and by embracing your power and talents, freeing up any need to control, reacquainting yourself with the innate power you were born with, and standing back to measure your personal aspirations against the highest good of all involved.

Encourage forward movement by asking: What does accepting my power mean to me? *List all those changes occurring in your life because you accepted your own power to work on your dreams.*

Don't be dismayed if this exercise takes you awhile. When I first sat down and really thought about tapping into and renewing my spirit power, and how I could change my life, I was a bit overwhelmed. I discovered that my concerns were mainly because I hadn't really consciously considered these concepts before. After some serious thought and many days of reflecting, these are the first results I came up with:

- ✯ I will have increasingly clear vision about what my biggest dream entails.

- ✯ I will gain increasing clarity on how I am to pursue it.

- ✯ My newly claimed income level will allow me to pursue my dream.

- ✯ My daily work will be congruent with my biggest dream.

Use the following heading to create a section in your journal to log in each day what changes occur as a result of accepting your fullest power: "All That Has Happened Since Accepting and Renewing the Power and Taking Total Responsibility for Making My Biggest Dream Come True."

Now, list all those things you've done. You might include:

✧ *I've established and now follow a schedule that suits me.*

✧ *I'm increasingly in touch with my inner spirit.*

✧ *This contact is creating an energy all its own.*

✧ *I've created an office/work/spiritual place just for me.*

✧ *My heart is lighter from knowing that I am working toward what I love.*

✧ *I am energized by working with people who believe in me and my dream.*

✧ *I am socializing with people with dreams of their own.*

✧ *I am asking for advice and guidance from experts whenever I know I want input.*

Note also how these changes will alter the lives of your family, cowork-ers, colleagues, fellow dreamers, and friends.

Watching the transformation that comes with people realizing and accepting increasing amounts of spirit and personal power is exhilarat-ing. Understanding that the realization of their biggest dream improves the world, they are even more effective than before. That's because they are not only sharing their dream, but also their enthusiasm and awareness, with those around them. By sharing our power, we enable ourselves to move through the open door and cross the threshold onto our dream path to live in discovery and celebration.

Never Again

Having completed this chapter, you have a better understanding of your power and ego, as well as everyone else's. If you choose, never again give your power away or desire to deplete or abuse others' either. As you address the following, think about what you really want to put behind you, even though it may seem difficult to do so right this minute. By making a commitment to change, you begin to rid yourself of limiting and self-depreciating behaviors. You begin to recognize what it really means to live from your fullest spirit power.

Begin to explore and gather information that empowers you to stay in your power. Make lists of what necessary dream steps you are ready to write down and fully embrace in order to celebrate your biggest dream.

_____

_____

_____

_____

_____

_____

_____

_____

_____

_____

_____

_____

_____

_____

_____

_____

_____

_____

_____

_____

_____

_____

_____

_____

_____

_____

_____

List the Web sites, current headlines, and book titles with which you identify now. Also tell why.

_____

_____

_____

_____

_____

_____

_____

_____

_____

_____

_____

_____

_____

_____

_____

_____

_____

_____

_____

_____

_____

_____

_____

_____

_____

_____

_____

List and then describe the times you have recognized your ability to practice using your personal and spirit power effectively and fairly.

_____

_____

_____

_____

_____

_____

_____

_____

_____

_____

_____

_____

_____

_____

_____

_____

_____

_____

_____

_____

_____

_____

_____

_____

_____

List the radio and television programs that are now drawing your attention. Also tell why.

_____

_____

_____

_____

_____

_____

_____

_____

_____

_____

_____

_____

_____

_____

_____

_____

_____

_____

_____

_____

_____

_____

_____

_____

_____

Describe the scenes or list the lines in films and plays that reflect your new view of yourself. Tell why.

_____

_____

_____

_____

_____

_____

_____

_____

_____

_____

_____

_____

_____

_____

_____

_____

_____

_____

_____

_____

_____

_____

_____

_____

_____

_____

_____

List and describe the powerful fictional people with whom your spirit power identifies.

_____

_____

_____

_____

_____

_____

_____

_____

_____

_____

_____

_____

_____

_____

_____

_____

_____

_____

_____

_____

_____

_____

_____

_____

_____

_____

_____

List and describe the powerful living people with whom your spirit power identifies.

_____

_____

_____

_____

_____

_____

_____

_____

_____

_____

_____

_____

_____

_____

_____

_____

_____

_____

_____

_____

_____

_____

_____

_____

_____

_____

_____

List and describe the people in your life right now who invite you into the laughter of discovery and thrill you with your loss of limits.

_____

_____

_____

_____

_____

_____

_____

_____

_____

_____

_____

_____

_____

_____

_____

_____

_____

_____

_____

_____

_____

_____

_____

Make the Dream Real...Make it Yours

Ego and worldly and spiritual powers are tangible. With awareness and conscious use you include them in your life's script. By doing that, you make them real.

You share your power when you say the following:

_____

_____

_____

_____

_____

_____

_____

_____

_____

_____

_____

_____

_____

_____

_____

_____

_____

_____

_____

_____

_____

_____

_____

_____

_____

_____

_____

You share your power when you take the following actions:

_____

_____

_____

_____

_____

_____

_____

_____

_____

_____

_____

_____

_____

_____

_____

_____

_____

_____

_____

_____

_____

_____

_____

_____

_____

_____

_____

_____

_____

_____

Rejoice and celebrate!

By sharing your dreams, you make them yours.

4

Crossing the Threshold

What I want most in the world is for everyone to be true to their dreams and work toward whatever it is they want to be and achieve. That's when everything begins functioning fittingly. That doesn't mean that there aren't challenges or down times, but overall, everything is working. When it doesn't, we need to pay close attention. It's our sixth sense alerting us to ask questions such as: *What am I learning right now? Am I on the path I need and want to follow? Is it time to reevaluate? Am I finished with this part of the dream? Is it time to change my direction or move on?* At this point, you are ready to move through the open door and across its threshold to a place where you further define what it is that you want. Expect, sometimes, to find illumination arriving in the most unexpected ways. I call this *living in the magic!*

I moved into and forward with my biggest dream because my granddaughter asked the question, "Grandma, am I going to be killed by a nuclear bomb?" Then she made a statement: "Gosh Grandma, if you can't end wars, no one can!" There it was: As a grandmother I had a responsibility to make our world safer for my grandchild. It is a responsibility that each of us carries. If we don't get on with it, there won't be any dreams for anyone! And so I began to take a self-inventory: Why was I on this planet at this time in history? What must I do to fulfill my own destiny so that my granddaughter might fulfill hers? It was up to me, I figured, to go higher and dream bigger. Although this might sound pretentious, or like a slogan for a New Age philosophy, for me, pushing myself to always "go higher" keeps me—and my personal dream—on track. It keeps me moving forward even when I might become lulled into inactivity by a temporary sense of fulfillment. Out of my inner pushing came a further definition of my biggest dream. Because I believe so completely that the salvation of the world depends upon the spiritual, physical, and emotional fulfillment of individuals, I was to begin to do what I needed to "save" the world for my granddaughter: assisting others, as well as myself, to fulfill our dreams.

You must understand that, except to my bemused husband, I made no such public announcement. The announcement I made to him, whenever he would ask where I was going was "I'm going out to change the world!" We would both laugh. It was not only fun but also empowering for me to claim my biggest dream in this way. With what I know about human nature, motivation, and commitment, I also knew that I could accomplish my biggest dream best by becoming a "dream coach." By inspiring, assisting, and empowering others to reach their destiny, I would also be realizing my own. Aligning our fulfilled energies, we would extend our enthusiasm to those around us. You know the rest: By sharing and following our dreams, eventually the entire world becomes a better place for all of humanity.

Moving Ahead:
A Personal Experience

Looking back on the last 20 years, my journey has been extraordinary. In my rearview mirror, I can see that by changing my profession from teaching to coaching, I simply enlarged my classroom. However, that's hindsight. Setting off on that first day, I had only a very rough map showing me where I was or indicating my destination. In between the two were many unfamiliar roads, paths, and byways. I think I took them all, and what I learned is that there were no dead ends. There were detours, however—and many unpaved roads instead of easy-to-travel super-highways. However, I found some of those routes to be blessings in disguise, for down some of the most unlikely paths I found unexpected learning, support, and guidance. Through discovery and loss, setbacks, and joys, I've gained a renewed sense of my spirit and myself. I've met so many marvelous people and now have new friendships and shared stories of dream journeys that I might never have known had I not slowed down long enough to take a more in-depth look at where I was, how I'd gotten there, and the determination of the route by which I would finally arrive.

Remaining in the Wishing Stage Gets You Nowhere—and Nothing

My mother had two dreams: to own a fur coat and to take a train trip across the United States. She did not realize either. Sure, rationing during World War II put a serious crimp in travel and the availability of luxury items, but that war ended when she was 45. And before the next one began, the economy was doing very well in providing her with a stable lifestyle and income. So it wasn't war, and it wasn't money that kept my mother from her dreams. It was remaining at the wishing stage— and reliance upon others to deliver her dreams to her doorstep—that kept that fur coat and dream trip "pie-in-the-sky" dreams. Don't allow yourself to put your dreams on hold! Cross the thresholds by taking charge of realizing your smallest and biggest dreams! Expect to celebrate!

Assuming Total Responsibility

Myra, a client in her mid-30s, was the pleasant young wife of a very successful man. On the surface, she shared that she had everything a person could want. Yet, she also said she'd joined my Live Your Dream workshop to get her dream life in order. Her dream? To continue to provide a stable and fulfilling life for herself and her children. When other group members discussed *living* their dreams, she said that she probably couldn't begin "until I get the laundry done!" Laundry? Doing the laundry was stopping her?

Instinctively, Myra knew that the current state of her house reflected the disorder in her entire life. So she had done the only thing that seemed sensible to her: She signed up for my workshop to learn *how* to restore order and find purpose in her life. With a clean and tidy house, she figured that her relationship with her family would improve and she could get on with her dream. Finally, she thought, she would be happy.

Realizing (from working with a group) that she needed more coaching at this stage in her life, Myra asked for a private coaching session in her home. It wasn't until I got there that I realized just how out of control things were. Rooms were in complete disarray. The laundry, clean and dirty side by side, took up an entire room and rose nearly to the ceiling.

Although Myra was quick to accept responsibility for having created the chaos, she wasn't certain until my visit that she could take charge. Except, this was a woman who had never *heard* the term "time management." Even making a list of what needed to be done seemed to be beyond her. Together, we discussed how we might get her home ready for a party. As she described her steps, I wrote them down. Then, we designed an efficient timetable for washing, drying, folding, and ironing clothes. The household budget allowed her to hire a cleaning service to come in each week to care for the rest of the house. In a rather short period of time, physical order was restored.

Myra then turned her attention to the yard, hiring a gardener to shape up the flowerbeds and keep the grass mowed and a handyman to finish uncompleted projects. With everything in good order, it was time for Myra to get on with the next step toward providing a stable environment for her children. But, with hours each day suddenly available, Myra had time to realize that it wasn't just an untidy house and yard that had been making her unhappy. It was her husband's frequent absences, her children's constant complaints, and the never-ending demands of her alcoholic parents and adult siblings. So Myra had to step aside and take a good look at what she had not wanted to see before. Only then could she begin to create another—better—reality.

As I've said, before we can change those around us—and the world— we must first change ourselves. And Myra did. Over the next two years she reviewed her childhood. Finding that, as many children of alcoholic parents do, she'd carried the uncertainties of her childhood into her adult life. Because she *never* knew what was expected of her, she rarely finished anything she started. Never having received coherent directions, she was incapable of giving them. Although her home was functioning much more smoothly, her children could still not expect meals to be served on time, if at all. It was the same in the homes of her parents, brothers, and sisters. On top of that, Myra had to accept another fact: Her husband was an alcoholic, too. If there was to be a stable environment, she alone had to provide it, which meant that she needed to find out what was "normal." Reading the self-help and child-development books I suggested, she then joined an Adult Children of Alcoholics support group. Working with school staff, she learned how to enforce normal disciplinary measures at home. By letting her children know that she was the parent and was in charge, she let them know that it was safe for them to be children. In other words, by becoming stable herself, Myra was living congruently with what she wanted in her life.

This has not been a quick journey. It took five years, a degree in business, detaching from her dysfunctional family, and a divorce for Myra to establish a well-functioning life. It hasn't been an easy journey, either. A romance with another alcoholic showed her how vigilant she must be not to repeat earlier mistakes. But what she's won is the respect and love of her children, self-respect, and wonderful reasons to get up in the morning. Was I disappointed when she told me she had entered into a new relationship with another alcoholic? Yes! But even dream coaches have lessons, and Myra has been in my life to illustrate that I could just as easily be pulled away from my own dream! I learned that I could continue to care with all my heart but it was best not to work with anyone who is not living congruently with what he or she says he or she wants to be, do, and have. Because my dream is to change the world by helping individuals attain their dreams, I stepped aside from Myra until she went back to taking the steps required to follow her dreams and to improve her life and her children's lives. With her dysfunctional relationship no longer in her life, she is ready to continue, and we are working together to align with her dreams. Harmful old habits and fear of change aren't for dream activators. Taking charge, clarity, and persistence are!

Persisting Allows for Small Successes Along the Way

Rick is a perfect example of someone who, by living congruently with his dream, has enjoyed many successes along his way. At the age of 25, Rick was unsure of what he wanted to do after college. What he liked to do most, he confessed, was play. At my suggestion, he listed all the things he considered "play." Then he listed the talents and abilities he possessed, along with all the skills he'd acquired from various jobs he'd held. Proudly, he rattled them off: He could read, write, talk, deliver papers, build houses, cook, wait tables, clean houses, fix any kind of plumbing, baby-sit, compete as a cross-country runner, play tennis, surf, windsurf, roller blade, and ski. What this list suggested was that he was well-equipped not only to play himself, but to teach others to play, as well. While still thinking this over, Rick had a fateful encounter on the beach after a day of surfing.

With his surfboard under his arm, Rick happened by a staged modeling "shoot." When it was over, he strolled over to the photographer and asked how a person got started in the modeling business. Automatically the photographer told him to get a portfolio of good head and action shots, and then find an agency to represent him. Asking for the man's card, Rick asked when he could call for an appointment. Barely looking up from what he was doing, the photographer said, "Tomorrow." The next morning when Rick called, the photographer was surprised. In his experience, he said, people rarely followed through on suggestions given. Having opened the door on a potential dream, Rick began the process of crossing a new threshold.

There followed years of reading, training, and traveling as Rick circled the world as a professional model. And, as happens when people are in total alignment with their natural talents and skills, new opportunities, new ideas, even new thresholds appeared. What Rick discovered was that the part of modeling that he enjoyed most was the performing part. Once again, he began reading up on what it took to be an actor. In the months that followed, he studied acting techniques used by actors in plays and films, and he began to concentrate on getting the modeling jobs that involved performing. What Rick discovered is that he could support himself in several ways—and in ways congruent with the life he wanted to lead—but not consistently. However, as Rick says, "If playing for a living was easy, everybody would be doing it!"

So, Rick, instead of stopping, getting too comfortable, or becoming complacent, took what he'd learned and moved on.

Rick's biggest dream was becoming clearer. Simply put, he wanted to live each moment of his life as fully as he could. He wanted to express himself congruently with who he was and what he knew. So, between assignments, Rick supported himself by waiting tables, got married, and continued to model and study acting. In the mid-1980s, he decided that he needed a firmer financial base. Returning to his hometown, he became the engaging managing partner in a very busy beach-city bistro. For Rick, running a business allows him to be who he is: friendly, compassionate, and helpful to patrons and staff alike. Being his own boss also allows him to continue to model and perform in local, semiprofessional theater. Is that congruent? Is it persistent? Well, his brother recently commented, "Rick, you're the only person I know that lives life as if it were a vacation!"

Going Beyond Initial Accomplishments

Speaking of small and large achievements and successes, sometimes what we consider small becomes a larger achievement or success for others as well. A former newspaper editor and his wife moved out of state upon retiring, intent upon hiding from the world. To keep himself occupied, Jim planted a vegetable garden, which produced beyond his wildest dreams. In a few months he was faced with a mountain of fresh produce. So, this man who sought time away from the formal service organizations of his professional past has returned to service—but in his way: Three times a week he packs boxes of fresh tomatoes, green peppers, and different varieties of lettuce, carrots, and cabbages into his truck and drives 50 miles to the nearest large city, where he donates it to a refuge for battered women and their children. That wasn't what he planned;

what he'd looked for was something to keep him physically and mentally alert. Does he celebrate his garden? You bet he does—every day of the week. Is he fully aware of the difference his contribution is making? Maybe not, and that isn't necessary. What is necessary, however, is that he activated his dream. Once activated, the dream expanded to meet the needs of others. Your dream, too, must involve your health, work, spiritual development, relationships, finances, and creative expression. By becoming all that you can be right now, you are able to become and do what you want tomorrow! What you may find is that your dream is benefiting not only you, but others as well.

That is certainly true for my 50-something client Francine, who thought it was time that she relax and enjoy her husband of 30 years. Unfortunately, he decided at the same time to leave her and start life anew with a younger woman. Destroyed, Francine took five years to even think about healing the wounds. She started that process when she moved away from her old hurts and pains. Settling in southern California, she met me through a local business owner. Unhappy enough to make an appointment, Francine enrolled in one of my journaling workshops to rediscover how she could recover her confidence and joy in living.

Through journaling and her commitment to creating a new life, Francine was inspired to seek out advisers to assist her. She consulted with a nutritionist to revise her health habits. After contracting with an image consultant, she began making outward changes that reflected what was going on inside. Changing her diet, updating her clothes and hairstyle, and learning how to apply fashionable make-up, Francine was soon looking and feeling like a new person. It was at this point that she first saw reason for a little joy and began to feel it, with a small group of friends. Not stopping there, she continued to attend lectures, read, use advisers when she felt it necessary, and journal to continue the growth she'd begun. Some of the advisors she hired were an investment counselor, a real-estate adviser, and a broker to manage property she'd inherited. With the completion of each step, she celebrated with an ever-expanding group of friends. Today, Francine is remarried and is an exceptionally happy woman who regularly contributes to local hospitals and the arts. She continues to celebrate each and every day. But she's not the only one—a *great many* people celebrate Francine's dream!

Taking Time to Think!

The people in the previous stories gave a lot of thought to who they were, where they came from, and where they were going. When was the last time you took time to examine what is going on in *your* life? In your head? In your heart? For that matter, when did you last spend an entire day by yourself? And when did you last spend an entire day *just thinking?*

All too few of us make time to just *be*, even when we know how important it is to sit in the silence and listen to what we are trying to tell ourselves. Because we have integrated earlier dreams into our day-to-day lives, we expect more of ourselves than ever before. That too often means that we are busier than ever and have not stopped to take more than 15 minutes or half an hour to reflect. Yet, if we are to continue activating our dream by crossing the threshold into new experiences, we need to dedicate more thinking and reflecting time *each day* to assess where we are! By avoiding or not doing so, we may be missing something.

Take the next half hour to begin thinking about where you want to be in the next six months. Then open up your journal and record your thoughts and feelings. Are you ahead of schedule? Or is it time to move on?

Taking More Time to Think and Dream

Answers to questions such as the ones you just answered may require even more time, possibly many weeks of contemplation. That means developing a new habit of regularly scheduling time away from the phone, friends, family, associates, and regular activities. It means retreating to a place of tranquility, whether that means a week at a spa; a drive in the country; or a visit to an art gallery, museum, forest, monastery, desert, seashore, library, or the middle of a cornfield—wherever *you* find serenity.

Arrange your schedule so that you can spend one, two, or three days in that peaceful place. When you go, be sure to take your journal, your art pad, and any other equipment or supplies to capture your thoughts and feelings.

Dreaming Big Dreams: Yours and Others

While you were thinking, did you ask yourself if the dream you are working on is yours or someone else's? This is a question I'm often asked. You know intuitively if you are following your own dream or supporting someone else's! And, you may be realizing that, to reach your own dream, you may *have* to work on someone else's first. A good example might be this: If you want to be mayor of your city, you may need to work to support the current mayor to learn the ropes and build up a constituency. It is vital that you really *do* support the current mayor, of course. To support someone you do not believe in or respect is, of course, living incongruently with your own highest standards. On the other hand, you might enter politics to discover if this is *really* your dream by supporting that mayor *without* having a plan to succeed him or her. Is there a hard-and-fast rule by which you always know what your next step is going to be? No. Not always. Each of us is different, and so are our individual circumstances. Whenever you feel *alive* when working on a dream—yours or someone else's—you are at that moment traveling the right path. Just be aware that when your personal passion is not aroused, or begins to fade, the dream you are giving your energy to may not be related to your own.

Another way to know if you are working toward achieving your biggest dream is to ask yourself if you are operating in your own personal and spirit power or in someone else's. If you are subordinating your powers to someone else—or to a company, organization, or movement—you will always feel that something is missing. It may appear as a sense of loss, a recurring illnesses, stress, vague discontent or unhappiness. This happens all too often in the workplace, where having an income may be taking precedence over what we *really* want to do. Frequently, we started out enthusiastically learning all that we could learn on that job. But years of repetition, or maturation and personal growth taking us beyond confines of our workplace, has led to our emotional and creative burnout.

Mothers, fathers, caregivers, and even grandparents too often minimize personal dreams to give time and effort to dependents. Although "living for others," sounds terribly noble, it doesn't have to be a permanent extension of being a provider. Raising healthy, happy children to responsible adulthood is, indeed, a virtuous accomplishment—as long as it isn't a substitute for getting on with personal development. Not to do so makes living for others cowardly instead of righteous. Just as detrimental are the cases where children are expected to live a parent's dream. The results of that are to be seen in the acting out of the offspring of the rich, influential, and powerful, even as adults. Robbed of their right to have a dream of their own, to choose, and to experience personal fulfillment, they are without purpose. Everyone must be allowed to live in his or her own power. Everyone needs his or her own dreams, his or her own personal stage and spotlight.

For some, destiny *does* lay in carrying on a dream for someone else or supporting someone else's dream. Natalya Solzhenitsyn, wife of Russian author Alexander Solzhenitsyn, is a fine example of someone who understands direction in the role she takes in another person's life. When asked by a television interviewer how she viewed herself in relationship to her famous husband, she replied that she loved his work. It appears that *her* work is making sure that he receives the support to get his work done and that will provide fulfillment for her creative expression.

Graphing Your Way to Knowing Whose Dream You're Pursuing

Having elected to cross the threshold to a new dream, let's measure the time and commitment you are spending on its fulfillment. Keep track of the minutes and hours—in 15-minute segments—you spend thinking about, planning, or actively pursuing a dream for a 24-hour period. I recommend doing this exercise for at least a month—or until you know that you are on your own personal dream path (or someone else's).

Select one color to represent time spent thinking and/or time spent actively pursuing the dream you're working on. Begin charting upon awakening each day, and end when you go to bed.

AM ————→ PM ————————→ AM ——→

Minutes	5	6	7	8	9	10	11	12	1	2	3	4	5	6	7	8	9	10	11	12	1	2	3	4
15																								
30																								
60																								

Your graphing shows you how much time and energy you are expending on a current dream step. What did you feel whenever you logged that time onto the graph? Challenged? Elated? Thrilled? Energized? Then you are living your dream!

Did you avoid logging the time on the graph? Did you feel discomfort or resistance? Did you experience physical symptoms of illness? If so, you are probably living up to someone else's expectations or dreams.

For those of you actively pursing your own personal dream, there are more questions: Do you need to make changes in the way you direct and use your time? Perhaps what you need is to reduce/eliminate activities and practices that conflict with the mental image you have of living and celebrating all your dreams. As you rid your life of non-dream-related duties, the closer you come to making your biggest dream a reality.

Replacing the Old With the New

If you're stuck on knowing what to replace the non-dream activities with, consider introducing yourself to new activities or surrounding yourself with new groups of people or changing jobs. How about going back to school, losing 15 pounds, gaining 15 pounds, studying a new philosophy or metaphysics, traveling, coloring your hair, stopping coloring your hair, going back to playing the clarinet, being the only 45-year-old man in a beginning ballet class, auditioning for a part in community theater, volunteering for a worthy cause or charity, becoming a foster parent or big brother/sister, running for office, bicycling across the country, taking up weaving, joining the Peace Corps, taking up skydiving, entering a marathon, or ending old relationships or beginning new relationships. Begin to *stretch* your brain, your emotions, and your body. By investigating new habits and practices related to your biggest dream, your interests grow. In stimulating your interests to things beyond what you've been doing, you move forward. In moving forward, you meet new people, learn new skills, and enjoy life more. All this brings you closer to living in celebration.

Running Into Your Fears

"But," you object, "what if I choose the wrong thing? I haven't got time for mistakes." Let me tell you about a marketing specialist who came to me. She said that she knew exactly what she wanted and how fast she wanted to get it. She was a bright, assertive young woman who had already achieved considerable success and was eager to take the next step to a new and bigger dream.

During our first session, she established what she wanted and her time line for meeting those goals. Together, we drew up a list of what needed to be done. She rapidly completed the first week's tasks and assignments. The second week, she did most of them. The third week—well, the third week she didn't do anything. As her coach, it was my responsibility to find out why. Here were my questions, and her answers.

Were the tasks or assignments she'd picked too difficult? "No!" she replied.

Had she failed at anything she'd undertaken so far? "No!" she quickly replied.

Then what was holding her back? After a long, contemplative pause, she confessed, "It's going too fast!"

She was and always had been an achiever; she'd accomplished many of her earlier dreams in record time. And this was *her* schedule we were meeting. She had come to realize that she was afraid that she hadn't had the foundation or appropriate training to be as powerful as she wanted to be. Never had she pressed herself to stretch this far or this fast before. Not only that, but up to this point she'd had models to imitate and other people's dreams to follow. Although her dream was to go farther than anyone else had gone, *pioneering* a role required that she step into a mental and emotional void. What she'd have to do is create new guidelines. Even scarier, it might mean admitting to others that she didn't have all the questions, much less all the answers. Overwhelmed by these realities, she pulled back. Right now, she says she's hit a dead end. In reality, she's only taken a detour. That is all right—as long as comfort doesn't permanently keep her there.

Remember Linda, the New York editor who moved to California to start her own freelance editing business? She says that with all of her big-city-publisher experience, she remained in her job for nearly three years past the time she wanted to leave. Why? Fear. Fear that her New York associates would think she was leaving because she couldn't "cut" it anymore. Fear that, maybe, she wouldn't make it. How could she explain that to family and friends? Now that she's overcome all that, she's looking toward another dream: establishing a home for battered women for her part of the city. And guess what? The same old fears are surfacing again. What will people think? Will she compromise her income to the point she has to back out? Funny how old fears crop up, even when we're at our most successful in life. This is why it's so important to keep seeking clarity about what you want. The soul-searching you do will lead you to uncover your fears and hesitations and meet them face to face.

Getting Clarity Through Self-Inventory

The average person requires some professional help, guidance, or advice at some time in his or her life. However, before you rush out and buy training videos, enroll in college, get a bank loan, or engage a financial advisor, a broker, or investment counselor, there are decisions that only you can make. After determining precisely what your biggest dream is going to require, you might find that you require a dream coach or a professional recruiter. For someone who wants to be a physician, this may mean not only bank loans, but the support of an entire community to whom the future doctor pledges the first five years of his or her medical career. For a person who wants to be a model, dental work might be required, along with acting classes, photographer fees, and an agent. Whatever it is you want, or want to be, observe everything you can about people who are already there. As Socrates wrote, "The unexamined life is not worth living." Before you determine what type of assistance you might want, let's examine more specifically what else you may need to advance yourself and to move forward to your biggest dream.

Mark what you want and need to achieve your next dream steps and to achieve your biggest dream.

❏ Motivational tapes.

❏ Meditation tapes.

❏ Books/libraries.

❏ Self-inventory.

❏ College degree.

❏ Mentor.

❏ Gardener.

❏ Hypnotherapist.

❏ Massage therapist.

❏ Housekeeping/cleaning service.

❏ Vocational education/ training.

❏ Counselor/therapist/ psychiatrist.

❏ Exercise coach.

❏ Consultant/trainer.

❏ Image consultant.

❏ Marketing firm.

❏ Secretarial services.

❏ Financial advisor.

❏ Physician.

❏ Nutritionist.

❏ Party consultant.

❏ Attorney.

❏ Travel adviser.

❏ Literary agent.

❏ Video-feedback consultant.

❏ Publicist.

❏ Postgraduate education.

❏ Childcare/nanny.

❏ Voice coach.

❏ Speech coach.

❏ Dream coach.

❏ Personal-growth consultant.

❏ Movies/plays/musical or artistic events.

❏ New or expanded empowerment group.

❏ On-the-job-experience/ apprenticeship.

❏ Certification for _____ .

❏ Other _____ .

❏ Other _____ .

❏ Other _____ .

❏ Other _____ .

❏ Other _____ .

❏ Other _____ .

Special-interest classes/workshops:

❏ Acting/drama.   ❏ Musical instruction.

❏ Assertiveness.   ❏ Painting/drawing/sculpture.

❏ Parenting.   ❏ Classes on play/fun/humor.

❏ Communication skills.   ❏ Dance/movement/aerobics.

❏ Personal growth.   ❏ Other _____ .

❏ Financial planning.   ❏ Other _____ .

❏ Journaling.   ❏ Other _____ .

Aligning With What You Want and Need

Having crossed the threshold, you may now be entering unknown territory. Depending upon what you checked on the list, you may need one or more experts or guides. Going it alone can be scary—maybe even overwhelming! To put those concerns in their appropriate perspective, dream activators know that help is everywhere. This calls for another step aside, because you certainly don't need to know everything. You can arrange for, or hire, what you want and need to get to where you want to be. Designing a "plan of action" is what comes next.

Start to develop your plan of action by writing down the things you checked in the previous section in the order that you intend to use them. Then, as this listing is necessarily linear, send yourself beyond its sequential thinking by doing cluster designs, doodles, and drawings in your journal or on your art pad. If you've listed motivational tapes, for example, then draw or paste on a picture of a video or audio tape. Illustrating each of your steps stirs the subconscious, awakens your spirit power, and is quite simply more fun! By doing this, you are aligning with your biggest dream. Sign up for the classes you've identified with, interview the professionals you're going to need, and get going! Then, keep your diagram and lists available and continuously update by adding or deleting! Be sure to let your fellow dreamers join you in the learning and the experiences!

Anyone who or anything that is not on the list but is in your life may no longer be necessary. Living true to yourself and your biggest dream will require that you fully embrace constantly changing and evolving. Practicing a habit, meeting with people, or participating with anything that changes your focus disempowers your life and your dreams.

Telling Your Own Truth to Further Empower Your Biggest Dream

Very, very few people tell themselves the whole truth, although each of us has his or her own truth. Primarily this is communicated through language, both verbal and body. Remember back when you knew what you wanted to do and say! Although it was appropriate for your authority figures to make you acceptable for society, they may also have dampened your spirits and harnessed parts of you, including what you said, that are now perfectly appropriate for you to think, feel, or say.

Go back and observe that free-spirited and carefree child that you were. Ask yourself what you would have thought about your biggest dream back then. How would you have described your life as you envisioned it? What would you have claimed to make it all come true? Capture those feelings and words so that you aren't saying what you think other people want to hear or limiting them to what you think is or is not possible. Express what you think about your biggest dream in writing as honestly and purely as you would have when you were a child. Record all that you are now seeing for yourself and continually reinforce your truths as you discover and rediscover them!

Dream activators learn not to allow false politeness to remain a part of their lives. That means that once you become a person who is committed to a task, you can no longer put up with behaviors (your own or anyone else's) that are incompatible with what you are trying to become or achieve. At the same time, there is no room to direct blame, shame, or guilt at yourself or others. From the moment you assume absolute responsibility for the realization of your dream, you can blame no one else for difficulties encountered. Accept problems and know the freedom that comes from knowing what you want; the emancipation that comes from working toward getting it. So, once you've uncovered that dream, let others know of your intent. When you align with what you want, your dream should be a secret no more.

Does this mean you should be rude, cruel, or thoughtless? Absolutely not! Never! Certainly, being diplomatic aids others in understanding what your newly announced needs and ideas are; even better, when you live your dream, you free those around you to express themselves and live their dreams, too. By coming out and saying what you are thinking, you create opportunities for others to do the same. By following your example, they may reexamine their lives and grow, too. Get into the habit of allowing yourself to *feel* everything! Think everything. Avoid nothing, and when you see and hear *your* truth, align with it and speak it freely. Liberated from everything holding you back, you can get on with the work of manifesting your dream. Experience the moment: If you are happy, be happy! If you are sad, know that *it is all right* to be sad. If you feel passionate about something, experience the fervor and express it appropriately. If you want and need support, reach out and find it through empowering people and experiences.

Placing Yourself in Empowering Environments

John loves Dixieland music. For years, he attended local sessions and three-and-a-half-week-long band concerts throughout the state, but what he really wanted was to be personally involved. Unfortunately, he could neither sing nor play an instrument well enough to be considered band member material. John has now found a way to become involved anyway: by volunteering to man the tape sales booth several hours each day during local events. Is he satisfied? Not completely, because what he'd really like to do is solo on the trumpet in public. Because of his current level of expertise, he only accompanies taped tunes at home. John finds that even his clandestine bugling is more fun now, because most of the Dixieland amateurs and professionals he works with recognize the contribution he makes in selling their tapes. Their thanks give him cause to celebrate his decision to join them and claim them as part of his empowerment team. They take time to encourage him to continue practicing and celebrating his love of music, too. So if you love—and have little talent for—barbershop singing, opera, fine art, or writing, find a way to align with those who do: Sell or take tickets, usher, become a docent, collect information for a newsletter, be on a telephone committee, or help in money-raising efforts to support your favorite group. It takes more than outstanding talent to keep the dreams alive, so get moving in the right direction with the right people. Taking action empowers you—and all of your dreams.

In the same way, if your dream is to become a thoracic surgeon and you have yet to start medical school, volunteer at a hospital where you will associate with people already working in your field. If, for another example, you wish to use your art training to become a full-time book illustrator, attend writers/illustrators conferences offered through college and university extensions to learn who in the publishing business can give you some direction. If owning your own business is your dream, make an appointment with the Small Business Association and get a mentor. Attend local chamber of commerce meetings. Join and become active in local, state, and/or national service groups. Whatever your interest, go on the Internet and start your research! Find the resources that are now available to fulfill you needs. By activating even the first stages of your biggest dream, your take charge of your future. The people you connect with will become an empowerment team. Even though you may never meet formally, the interest and alignment will often be the needed spark to ignite your spirit power.

Using Your Empowerment Team

Although having a group of special people in an empowerment team is always an ongoing desire, most people find that groups frequently provide more support than direction. Although they may no longer be able to contribute what you need as you move on, members of your groups are tremendous co-celebrants. Virginia has the voice of an angel. At the urging of a neighbor, she tried out for a prestigious local choir. She did and against tremendous competition, she won a place in the soprano section. The next few months were spent preparing for a citywide concert, but when Virginia tried to get her family to attend the concert, everyone was too busy. When she called the neighbor who'd started the whole thing, the neighbor had previous plans. Virginia sang that night in the choir, but she dropped out the following week. Why, when she enjoyed it so? Because part of her enjoyment came from having her family and friends enjoy her triumph with her. What Virginia needed was an empowerment team outside of her family and immediate friends. Without anyone to appreciate her and the music she helped create, it wasn't worth it to her to continue. You may be curious whether the rest of her life is fulfilling. As you might suspect, it's full of compromises. And the voice that could have lifted her out of compromise has been silenced for now, a voice that might have comforted some, entertained many, and inspired still others to pursue their own dreams. When a dream dies, everyone loses.

Cheering and Sabotaging Sometimes Come in the Form of Support

On the other hand, be forewarned that false cheering can often be just as destructive as no cheering at all. How many times have you, or people you know, been "comforted" after a setback with, "That's all right, honey. I still love you!" Would that person still have loved "honey" if he or she had succeeded?

That type of statement is akin to the dozen roses that are supposed to make up for cruel words or thoughtless behavior. Those posies are nothing but betrayal's mask, yet false support like that can be very seductive. Enough of it and a person begins substituting false praise or support for real support—for a while. Eventually, the thrill of the new possession or gift wears off and the recipient feels a return of emptiness. So make certain that you are truly supported by those around you. What would a supportive person say to a partner who failed? "It's only a setback" or "I have every faith in your ability to win next time." A fellow dream activator says, "How about if I take over some of your responsibilities to give you some extra time to focus and work towards your biggest dream?" or "Let's design a plan that will free to do the research to build a foundation for your biggest dream!" That's real empowerment; know the difference!

Identify the Characteristics That Empower You

Now that you know better what you might need, I want you to be clear about the characteristics you want in those on your empowerment team, in your circle of dreamers, and in every aspect of your life. Realization of your dream often depends a great deal on the personality and habits of those who empower, assist, and surround you.

Read over the following lists. Check off the characteristics that you think are important for your empowerment. After all, what could be more important than having the type of guidance that brings you into celebration?

❏ Single.

❏ Male.

❏ Female.

❏ Young.

❏ Old.

❏ Humorous.

❏ Curious.

❏ Generous.

❏ Married.

❏ Professionally successful.

❏ Creative.

❏ Happy.

❏ Optimistic.

❏ Powerful.

❏ Courageous.

❏ Stimulating.

❏ Honest.

❏ Congruent.

❏ Intelligent.

❏ Perceptive.

❏ Conscious.

❏ Disciplined.

❏ Visionary.

❏ Tidy/orderly.

❏ Accurate.

❏ Organized.

❏ Physically attractive.

❏ Nurturing.

❏ Adventuresome.

❏ Dependable.

❏ Religious.

❏ Spiritual.

❏ Psychic.

❏ Personally successful.

❏ Dedicated to helping me make my dreams come true.

❏ Other _____ .

❏ Other _____ .

❏ Other _____ .

❏ Other _____ .

Talking About Your Dream Gives It a Power of Its Own

By now, you probably have the confidence to enjoy living in the reality you've created by crossing the threshold of your dream toward your life's work. Talking to your fellow dreamers, friends, family members, and colleagues about your biggest dream is part of what has become natural.

The following questions are wonderful to include in your daily thinking, as well as in any and all conversation:

★ What is your biggest dream?

★ What did you do today to realize your dream?

★ What action steps are you taking to reach your dream?

★ What did accepting your power mean to you at this stage of your life?

★ How did accepting your power enhance someone else's life?

★ What smaller dreams are you realizing?

★ How did you celebrate each one of them?

★ Have you identified any additional challenges and opportunities?

★ What is your plan for managing them?

★ Are you finding/needing a coach/adviser/mentor?

★ How will using a coach/adviser/mentor further empower you?

✯ What steps are you taking to further empower your dream?

✯ What changes are you experiencing?

✯ Which parts of your life are congruent with your dream? Which are not?

✯ Are you jumping eagerly out of bed each morning?

✯ What new people are in your life? Describe them.

✯ What new things are in your life?

✯ What did you do today that made your heart sing and your spirit soar?

✯ Are you finding yourself thinking and acting more creatively now?

✯ How has moving into your dream changed your outlook on life?

✯ How has moving into your dream changed your outlook on *you*?

As you get together with empowerment group members, friends, and family, it might be inspiring for all of you to ask these questions of each other. As time goes on, you will undoubtedly add questions to the ones suggested here. Talking about all your dreams empowers you, and others, too—especially when you must combat the biases and setbacks of non-dreamers who proudly believe that they, and they alone, live in the real world.

Never Again

Having crossed the threshold, never again will you perceive limiting people or surroundings as restrictive. Nor will you remain for long in an environment that restricts or depletes your creative energy and spirit. As you address the following, think about what "crossing the threshold" really means to you, and notice this new concept taking form in your own world. Write about how crossing each new threshold allows you to more fully embrace your biggest dream.

List what you are suddenly noticing now that would have missed your attention before.

_____

_____

_____

_____

_____

_____

_____

_____

_____

_____

_____

_____

_____

_____

_____

_____

_____

_____

_____

_____

_____

_____

_____

_____

_____

_____

Notice and list the radio and television programs that you enjoy and find to be congruent with your dreams. Write why you are scheduling them into your weekly activities.

_____

_____

_____

_____

_____

_____

_____

_____

_____

_____

_____

_____

_____

_____

_____

_____

_____

_____

_____

_____

_____

_____

_____

_____

_____

Describe the "crossing the threshold" scenes in movies, plays, excerpts from books, and so forth that parallel the steps you are taking.

_____

_____

_____

_____

_____

_____

_____

_____

_____

_____

_____

_____

_____

_____

_____

_____

_____

_____

_____

_____

_____

_____

_____

_____

_____

_____

List and then describe the people who have supported you during the testing of your dedication to achieving your biggest dream.

_____

_____

_____

_____

_____

_____

_____

_____

_____

_____

_____

_____

_____

_____

_____

_____

_____

_____

_____

_____

_____

_____

_____

_____

List and describe the people who cheer you on and join with you to celebrate who you are and where you are going.

_____

_____

_____

_____

_____

_____

_____

_____

_____

_____

_____

_____

_____

_____

_____

_____

_____

_____

_____

_____

_____

_____

_____

_____

_____

_____

_____

Make the Dream Real...Make it Yours

You are fully aware of the current thresholds to be encountered and crossed. You step over them with awareness. Add celebration, adventure, and commitment to your script.

Write about how adding new elements to your life strengthens and empowers you and all your dreams.

_____

_____

_____

_____

_____

_____

_____

_____

_____

_____

_____

_____

_____

_____

_____

_____

_____

_____

_____

_____

_____

_____

_____

_____

Rejoice!

You know that from this point on, all thresholds will be congruent with achieving your biggest dream.

Living Your Dream in the Real World

5

Despite being in closer touch with our inner and outer selves, we may still encounter old obstacles with new appearances and often some new challenges as we progress. So I want to address the tough times that are bound to occur.

First, of course, you have to recognize tough times when they are upon you. You are probably asking, *How can I miss a setback, a change, a delay, or a problem?* Amazingly enough, sometimes it's easy. By way of explanation—and warning—I must tell you that one of the most paralyzing times can come with getting too comfortable. To illustrate: If you haven't completed a task or a dream step and things are going along so well that you just want to sit in the sun and enjoy yourself, chances are that you're avoiding, or not realizing you may be facing, one of your biggest challenges!

What's wrong with a little rest and relaxation? Nothing! Resting and relaxing are extremely important and likely directly related to your biggest dream. Just don't lull yourself into thinking that a momentary rest is fulfillment. Whenever your life becomes too comfortable, take a closer look at yourself; it's extremely difficult to move beyond contentment. Therefore, any time that you are feeling really satisfied, check to make sure your forward movement hasn't come to a standstill. If it has, sitting in the sun isn't bringing you any closer to your dream.

To get back on track, know that if you are to reach your dream, even vacations or lying-around times should be directly related to it. For instance, if sitting in the sun is part, or all, of your dream, and that's what you are doing, *celebrate!* If your dream is to write a book and you take a month off to think about it, *celebrate!* However, if your dream is to build a new winter resort, it may not further you to take a summer vacation in Florida, unless, of course, that's where you are finding investment capital or something else related to making your resort a reality. Dream activators enjoy a lot of things on the way to fulfilling their dreams, and they never allow themselves to lose sight of what they are doing on the way to where they are going. So beware of comfort and taking a vacation away from realizing your dreams!

Standing Aside

To have a better understanding of your comfort level, practice observing and viewing your present situation as an outsider. In that way, you get a clearer picture of what's really going on. What you want to identify is:

★ How many times a week are you thinking and acting as if you are already in the next stage of your biggest dream?

★ How often each day are you assuming you are living according to that dream?

★ How many times an hour are you aware of—and living according to—your biggest dream?

Actively living your dream by regularly thinking, behaving, and sounding as if it has already been accomplished allows you to be what you are seeking to become. Although everything in your life is neither finished nor completely resolved, it's getting better. Don't get distracted by that. Lingering in "getting better" can easily become *comfortable.*

Standing and stepping aside is an ongoing process; there will always be something to detach yourself from, always something more to examine, to learn, to experience. Simply attaining the years needed to be classified as an adult doesn't automatically provide you with complete knowing, understanding, insight, happiness, or the skills and methods to achieving and celebrating your dream. It takes conscious diligence to become an actualized dream activator.

Take time to write answers to the following questions in your journal:

✧ *What in my life do I want and need to detach from?*

✧ *What do I want to replace it with?*

✧ *What is my plan, and when do I intend to start?*

✧ *Can anyone in my empowerment team advise me? Who?*

These are questions you will be asking yourself throughout your life, so my advice to you is to answer them whenever you face a potential need to step aside. You will benefit if, at those times, you review what previous answers you gave; they may often serve as reminders and continue to give you direction.

Slipping Back Into Old Habits, Beliefs, Behaviors, and Patterns

Every day remind yourself that your biggest dream belongs to you. Create a visual affirmation that reminds you to keep this dream alive! Write your dream statement on your mirror! Hang an object that catches your attention whenever you enter your workspace, or make a collage and frame it! Stimulate yourself all the time! No one else can own it, and no one can take it away—unless you let him or her do so. By relaxing her vigilance my client, Carly, knew that her entire family was jeopardizing her dream journey.

Several years before, she had realized that if she were ever to have a life of her own she would have to break away from her dominating parents and incessantly complaining, needy brothers and sisters. So Carly moved 1,500 miles away, established herself professionally in a new city, met a wonderful man with similar goals, and married him. For a short time, Carly's life was her dream come true. In the first years of their marriage, she and her husband established habits that they planned to enjoy all their lives, simple things such as walking to a local bakery to buy fresh croissants on Friday evenings, then lying in bed Saturday morning reading the paper and drinking coffee and nibbling pastry until noon. In the bliss of living a life of her own design, she forgot about the daily conflict she'd endured before. Then, one by one, and two by two, her siblings and their mates followed her example. Inspired by Carly's obvious successes in her chosen city, they purchased homes a few miles away.

Although it was intrusive enough to suddenly begin receiving their daily phone calls and drop-in visits, it soon got worse. Carly's parents decided to move, too. All the conflict, the family upstaging, and sabotage that Carly had escaped was now once again in her world. Because she and her siblings had never given up their roles of obedient children, their parents expected everything to go on as before.

To Carly, their presence required accepting her old role of proving by daily action her gratitude for their "giving up everything" to send her through college. Despite the demands of her job, a new baby, a husband, and things around her own home to do, Carly felt obliged to go to her parents' house several evenings a week and weekends, either to visit, or to drive them places because they weren't used to freeways. It should come as no surprise that, within a few months, Carly had lost a significant amount of weight and was crying at the anticipation of having the phone ring.

One morning, when her son was nearly a year old, Carly awoke with what was becoming a standard headache. This time, with it came a thought: *I'm sick and tired of being pulled this way and that. I want my own life back!* Carly sought help from a professional therapist, who told her to step aside and reevaluate her entire family: her parents' role in her life, and her role in theirs. She made a decision to mentally remove herself from the family—to envision what her parents would do if she weren't around.

What Carly came to realize is that simply by participating in her parents' expectations, she had become part of the problem. To get back to living her own life, Carly had to quit what she was doing. She began by not reacting to her siblings' complaints or her parents' calls for help. Was it easy? Carly says that breaking those lifetime habits was the hardest thing she's ever done. To get her own dream back, though, it was something she had to do. What's happened since she began backing away from daily, then weekly, obligations? Now, her parents drive themselves, and Carly has had time to look at what she wants to do with the hours she's won back. She's pursuing her dream of becoming a lyricist, so she's taking music lessons, practicing her guitar, taking weekend retreats with her husband and baby, and spending time alone. By moving beyond old habits, beliefs, behaviors, and patterns, Carly's dream is expanding and she is celebrating!

Whenever you find yourself slipping back into old habits, beliefs, behaviors, and patterns, it is vital to reassess, to revitalize, the *new* you. Continue to review what you have recorded in your workbook, and write in your journal about the relationships, places, or things that no longer represent the person that you are becoming—or that will empower you to realize your biggest dream. In which areas do you need to move? Changing jobs? Reexamining personal or professional relationships? Seeking out expert advice? Establishing a support system for yourself?

Attitude Magic

For you maybe all it takes to feel as if your life is fulfilling is a refocusing of what's going on in your life at that moment. Although Carly needed to make some changes in her life to feel really fulfilled, sometimes it's just our outlook on life that can be detrimental to us living our dream. Indeed, after she examined her attitude, she found that her perception of and approach to her daily living situation was affecting her happiness as much as the situation itself was.

The following affirmations work on adjusting your attitude. Through engaging in a little "attitude magic" you might find that your life only needs some fine-tuning.

More than anything else, it is my attitude, or mental position, that ensures my ability to realize my dream.

★ ★ ★ ★ ★

My attitude toward life determines life's attitude toward me.

★ ★ ★ ★ ★

My attitude toward others determines others' attitudes towards me.

★ ★ ★ ★ ★

Gandhi said, "You must be the change you wish to see in the world." I think, act, talk, walk, and conduct myself in all my affairs as the person I choose to become, living in the world I choose to live in.

★ ★ ★ ★ ★

The deepest human desire is to be of service to others and to the world. I adopt an attitude of giving. I become an energy-giver, rather than an energy-taker, a constructive rather than destructive force in all my relationships.

★ ★ ★ ★ ★

I consciously work to develop a receptive mind. I learn from all my experiences. As I maintain an attitude of discovery, I know I unfold like a blossoming flower.

★ ★ ★ ★ ★

I radiate the attitude of well-being, of confidence, of someone who knows where I am and where I am going. I attract what I am.

★ ★ ★ ★ ★

My attitude determines my state of health and well-being. I focus on being healthy.

★ ★ ★ ★ ★

I focus on mental clarity and spiritual fulfillment. I focus on possibilities. I focus on my biggest dream.

★ ★ ★ ★ ★

If I don't have a dream, my life will be about problems. If I don't relate to others on the level of my biggest dream, my time will be occupied by my problems. By being creative, I create the life I want.

★ ★ ★ ★ ★

I nurture a positive attitude; I live in a positive world. For the rest of my life, I live the dreamer's life. I practice embracing and having a magical attitude.

★ ★ ★ ★ ★

I am what I dream. Shifting my attitude is a modern magic wand!

★ ★ ★ ★ ★

Moving Beyond Excuses

Reevaluating your life, or even looking at your present-day circumstances and finding out what is standing in your way can bring about mixed emotions. Although examining old behavior and habits that can be getting it in the way of you being all that you can be is often liberating, frequently the revelations bring us to a standstill. And then we find ourselves making excuses for not addressing them for not moving on.

A gifted writer stopped writing when she moved out of her parents' home because they had the computer. Believing that she could not write without a computer, she put her dream of being a novelist on hold. During a coaching session I pointed out that I'd written three books without owning a computer. Then I asked, "Have you always made excuses for not reaching a goal, a wish, or dream that you've said you want?"

"It's not an excuse! How can I write if I don't have a computer?"

"Many writers prefer to write in longhand. If you prefer to use a computer, consider renting one," I coached her. That was the end of that excuse! She had gotten into the practice of excusing herself. If writing is truly part of her biggest dream, she'd find a way! She needs to move through the excuses by making a list of all of the reasons that being a writer frightens her. It could be laziness, fear, or an unwillingness to tell herself the truth. Every dream activator needs to get in touch with the excuses he or she makes. Not taking responsibility for getting beyond them will make progress slower.

Take out your journal and make a list of how many socially acceptable excuses you have made this week, leaving a space between each one. Write about why you used them. In the space between each, describe what higher truth you could have told yourself and others. This habit will change your life, so continue to do this until you know you are always congruent.

Correcting Your Course When You Hit a Real-Life Barrier

Alice is an artist who had showings of her prints and oils in a number of states. When her first child was born, she began to find it difficult to schedule her need to paint with his nap times. Still, it was possible to think, experiment, and finalize a concept before the paint dried. Then came the second child! By the time her third child was born—11 months after the second—scheduling any time for herself became impossible. Alice's passionate need to create was stronger than ever, and her frustration about not filling the emptiness within her was making her frustrated and angry.

Realizing that she must find a solution, Alice decided to release her creativity in something that did not involve rapidly drying paint. Because she'd always loved to write, she bought a typewriter. "Rising each morning at 4:30 a.m. to write until 6:30 when my husband and children awake," she recently told me, "is wonderful. I'd found myself wanting to rush the children through things in the hopes of getting a few moments for myself. Now, I've had my creativity fix and, for the rest of the day, I'm able to relax and *enjoy* being a wife and mother. Each day is more fulfilling because I've allowed time for my dream of expressing myself and being creative." Remember: When you are fulfilled, everyone benefits!

Regrouping When Things Aren't Going the Way You Planned

Remember the Irish prayer that goes, "May the wind be always at your back"? Well, my dreams and I ran into some real challenging headwinds. In addition to the usual family losses, triumphs, and challenges, there came this:

After giving up my teaching career, creating a self-supporting business, and having my first book published, the recession hit California. Earlier, my husband had left teaching and coaching to enter into a partnership specializing in building spec houses. They'd constructed and sold four out of seven very expensive homes just before the floor dropped out from under the building industry. We'd never intended to sell one of the remaining three houses: That one was our dream home, the one in which I intended to live the rest of my life.

When notes came due on the last two houses and selling them appeared impossible, my husband and I were left to pay for the two partnership mortgages and the final sub-contractors' fees, along with our own mortgage and bills. Desperate to keep the bank from repossessing the two spec houses, we sold our home to partially pay debts incurred by the business. It turned out that our house didn't raise enough money, so we withdrew our retirement funds, canceled our private health insurance, and then added the small inheritance my husband had received from his mother. Finally, with only our furniture left, everything was paid off. Quite suddenly, there we were at retirement age with no pension, no investments, no home, and the dreams we'd held in our hearts. No doubt about it, this was definitely a tough time! Sometimes tough times are needed to find out who you are, what you stand for, and how important your biggest dream really is.

At the age of 63, my husband, no longer the owner of a construction firm, put on a carpenter's apron and headed for the one thing we still owned: a piece of property in another state. We hoped that we would recoup some of our losses by building and selling a house there. Then came time for my decision: With my company based and established in southern California, was I to accompany him and relocate my business?

As I saw it, to leave was to put a hold on living my dream. Reality was saying, *Pack it in: There's no extra money for an office, staff, or house rental.* But I knew better—I just felt it! First of all, I was willing to work 18 hours a day, if necessary. I was willing to go back to doing things the way I'd done them when I was first married. Moving into a tiny rental, I stayed to continue to write, create, and manage my business. Over the years, we'd become financially solvent enough that I'd purchased other people's services. Now, I did almost everything myself! It was both a wonderful and awful time. And on the most horrible, awful day that terrible year there came a sign that what I had done was right. My second book, *Journaling For Joy,* was published. And then *another* miracle happened in the form of confirmation: Letters began to arrive from all over the world from people who'd just purchased my second book to tell me how much my two books had changed their lives. After presentations and talks, people would come to me and thank me for rekindling shattered or delayed dreams, for motivating them to take responsibility for making changes in themselves. From this, I knew that I had been right to stay where I was: concentrating on the work that nurtured my spirit and continued to energize my dream.

Now there were, of course, other options. Both my husband and I could have gone back to teaching. In fact, many people suggested this. He could have taken any number of jobs right here in town, but he chose to go to a neighboring state. My choice was based on knowing that I am on this planet to help others discover their dreams and express myself through the work I love and am trained to do. Had I made excuses, moved at a time when my business needed my total commitment, or taken a job to help get us through, I might not now be writing this book, or perhaps the ones to follow. Because I regard remaining true to one's dream of ultimate importance, I want *you* to look upon any challenges coming your way as merely a signal that it is time to review—and then renew—your commitment to yourself and your biggest dream. That dream is your destiny. Claim it. Insist upon it!

And, there's always humor in the midst of hardship. While visiting the building site during a holiday, my husband was repairing damage on the third story of a house. Looking down at me from a 20-foot ladder, he yelled, "Joyce, I want you to know that I'm not *enjoying* my golden years!" True, things haven't turned out exactly the way we'd planned, but did we despair? Yes, of course! Have we given up? Never!

Daily Practices When You Get Stuck

Recently in one of my ongoing journaling groups a woman wrote about feeling stuck and remarked that it was time for her to "put on her power shoes." What she meant was stepping back into her personal and spirit power.

To get through being stuck, step into your power shoes. Then, take time to:

✦ Bring yourself back to center through realignment with your biggest dream.

    ★ Embrace living as if your dream is being realized.

    ★ Appreciate the little things that *are* working in your life by recording them in your workbook and journal.

    ★ Practice until you perfect the art of noticing the beauty of everyday things: sunlight coming through a window to splash across your desk, washing the car, the march of pansies along a path, the touch of caressing your favorite belongings, the musical tinkling of wind chimes stirred by the breeze.

    ★ Continue to replace any habits that reinforce lack of enthusiasm or that breed despair. This will lead to taking action that brings you closer to realizing and celebrating your biggest dream.

When Rita was being pressured to assume the presidency of a local historical society, I asked her what she really wanted to do. Having taken my Live Your Dream workshop, she had already partially identified a dream that would eventually affect everyone in the country: impacting the world through her writing. When she mentioned that she wanted time off from community responsibilities to plan that future, I asked a tongue-in-cheek question: "Well, can you be the president of the United States if you're busy being president of your local historical society?" Rita says that, as ridiculous a comparison as that was, it made all the difference in the world. "Suddenly everything was very clear," she said. "I could continue doing what I'd always done—which was very important on the local level—or I could recognize that now it's time to move forward." She not only removed herself from that organization, but Rita left another elected office and a part-time position as a college instructor.

Was it easy? No. Rita says, "Backing out on commitments is humiliating for anyone who prides themselves on being totally dependable." My response? "You might want to take a different view. Although all of those positions are extremely valuable, I don't see that you are deserting people. Instead, you are leaving positions that no longer fit with realizing your biggest dream." Did Rita have income to replace that which she gave up? Not within the next two weeks! However, believing that if she was working toward her own highest good, the highest-level authors and experts would come to her. Have they? Yes! Currently, she is ghosting a book for two psychiatrists and editing one for an attorney and another for a home nursing specialist. Will these books assist and empower others to change the world? Absolutely! In addition, Rita is experiencing the thrill of doing precisely what she knows she was put on this planet to do.

Ask and write about these questions in your journal daily:

- ✧ *What am I doing that is blocking my progress?*
- ✧ *What am I thinking that is blocking my forward movement?*
- ✧ *What am I willing to change or give up to follow my biggest dream?*
- ✧ *What is it that I must overcome?*
- ✧ *What is my plan?*

In addition, whenever I am blocked I repeat the following words, as many times as needed to get me where I want to be:

> I embrace and release all those past events, experiences, and beliefs that keep me from realizing my dreams. I send them toward the light with love, and thank them for what they have taught me.

By embracing, releasing, and acknowledging, I am free from any unneeded or unwanted influences.

Moving Beyond Giving Up

Each of us has had moments of glory. Despite that, however, we have at one time or another come to the point of giving up. Don't do that! Where there's a dream, there's a way, and, without a dream, no one is fully alive. Sitting here, writing and rewriting this book, it momentarily seems too demanding. But remembering the joy and the celebrations upon the publication of earlier books—and all the letters of gratitude that I've received—inspires me to go on beyond the frustration of *these* burdensome days and weeks. During times of tediousness, or fatigue, or hopelessness, I invite myself to recall earlier "moments of glory," and then write them all down. When you find yourself wanting to give up, or even postponing taking an action step, recall your moments of glory.

On your art pad or in your journal, list in chronological order your glorious moments and those who believed in you at the time: parents, coaches, mentors, teachers, friends, relatives, authority figures, or fellow dreamers. Reread and add to these often, until it is a habit for you to celebrate each and every dream step taken!

Phyllis knew from the time she was a child, retreating under the kitchen table with pencils and paper at age 6, that she was going to be a writer. Between that childhood and now, at 72, she has raised a family and worked in many jobs that always provided her with the opportunity to utilize her writing skills. Now as a semi-retired professional fund-raiser, she is putting the finishing touches on a novel.

Phyllis is one of those few fortunate souls who knew what she wanted to do at a young age. It also took her a whole lifetime to get back to her original dream. Although it's absolutely fine to live life and accomplish a whole host of other fulfilling tasks before you answer to your dream, it's magical how the heart's desire always surfaces and makes itself known.

Chances are that you had an inkling of what you wanted to do with your life early on. Maybe you ignored your dreams for a while. Maybe now you are coming into your dream late in life (and "late" is a relative term!). Or are you feeling stuck because you haven't yet listened to your innermost calling?

If you find yourself in a place where you feel like giving up, spend some time carefully examining the root of your biggest dream. You're sure to find that the seeds for those dreams were planted earlier in life, and perhaps some of your frustrations are simply the lack of attention to those dreams and their inability to surface.

- ✧ *Identify at what age you first knew the dream that you are working on now. (Phyllis was 6.)*

- ✧ *When were you first acknowledged for being able to do that? (Phyllis was in first grade when a teacher praised her stories.)*

- ✧ *What natural skills are you using? (Phyllis was a born writer, but she's never stopped honing her skills.)*

- ✧ *How are you now aligning with your dream? (Phyllis worked only in jobs directly involved in, or paralleling, her dream.)*

- ✧ *Are your feelings of being stuck or frustrated directly related to you not fulfilling your most coveted dreams?*

Moving Past the Advice and Opinions of Others

You've made up your mind. You are in the process of fine-tuning your plans and taking your latest step toward your dream. And then, for no apparent reason, you are stopped in your tracks by recalling the well-meant counsel or warnings of others. That is what happened to one of my clients, the owner of a charming specialty bookstore.

Previously, school-district librarian Karl had a 20-year history of depression and severe headaches. Since opening a specialty bookstore two years ago, he has been free of all illness. Although the shop supports his staff, the business will take a year or two more before it provides enough money to pay him an impressive salary. His retired teacher wife has complained since the bookstore opened that he was indulging in a whim, that he has had no background or training for developing a successful business. To exhibit her lack of faith in him, Helen insisted upon coming out of retirement and going back to teaching. However, the position she accepted was in another town some hundred miles away. To her, it made sense for them to move because hers was the job that was providing a steady income.

Unwilling to do this, Karl was nevertheless sensitive to his wife's needs. However, his bookstore wasn't losing money—and if Helen hadn't gone back to teaching, they would have had enough money in retirement funds to allow a certain amount of risk. But for Helen, who lives in what she considers to be "the real world," it seemed illogical to take these kinds of chances. Practical Helen is even willing to drive the 200 miles each day. Karl's brother sides with Helen. "You should be grateful to have a wife who is willing to safeguard your security," he told Karl. So, in addition to being a financial failure, it seems that Karl is ungrateful and selfish.

Will more explanation help Helen understand Karl's need to follow his dream, to test him—to grow? Just as important, without the challenge of making the bookstore a success, will Karl return to bouts of depression and debilitating headaches? He wonders. He also worries: Maybe Helen is right, and he is a terrible businessman. Maybe his brother is right: Is he foolish to endanger a marriage of 35 years? My recommendation is that Karl listen to *himself;* it is imperative that he determine what he *needs* as well as to know what he wants. Then, he is to acknowledge Helen for providing the stability that she needs to do for *herself!* He, after all, did not ask her to go back to work. He didn't even think it was necessary. Her peace of mind is important to him, so he has thanked her for what she is doing and continually acknowledges her for taking care of herself. At this point, Karl is not only doing that, he has also hired a business consultant to meet with him monthly for counseling and advice. Karl is, you see, every bit as practical as Helen. By listening to her and his brother, he realized that he might do more to guarantee the fulfillment of his dream.

Rarely do any of us progress without giving up something, and that is what Helen is doing, although she most likely doesn't know it. Helen's fear comes because Karl's idea of retirement turned out to be different from hers. After a year of staying around the house, he decided to do what he'd always wanted to do: open a small specialty bookstore. Threatened by this, Helen sincerely feels that she has to be the responsible one. Who else is going to take care of them, should his pie-in-the-sky dream not work?

For Helen, it is a matter of winning. If Karl continues to operate his bookstore, she is going to have to acknowledge that he is more capable, brighter, and has more business sense than she wanted to admit. She will observe this by watching how willing he is to make his dream come true.

Remember when I said that we must always work toward the betterment of all involved? If Karl gives in and gets rid of the bookstore, it is very likely that he will return to states of depression and debilitating headaches. To date, his decision is made. As Karl's dream coach, I'm confident that he will continue to follow his dream and celebrate along the way! Helen raises other questions. How soon will it be before she begins to resent spending four hours each day driving back and forth to work? Will she be able to see that she can join Karl in his dream by aligning with it? As a teacher, she is an expert in organization, creating exciting learning environments, and even in gift-wrapping purchased books. She created her part of the dilemma by jumping to the conclusion that Karl was jeopardizing their retirement funds. She is writing her own scripts, up until now, and I am hopeful that she will discover her own biggest dream. Learning what she wants and needs to know is her choice.

Learning to Prescribe for Yourself

Whenever you perceive something in your life to be a problem, shift your thinking and look at the situation as an opportunity, a lesson, or an exercise in learning. Once you understand what you are learning, move on. In the future, you must always first identify the lesson, determine what is to be learned, then prescribe how you're to use the lesson, and continue your journey. The important thing to remember when it is your lesson is that you are the only one who has the final answers. No one else in this world knows better than you what's in your heart and what will lead you to your biggest dream.

In a moment of desperate whimsy back when my life seemed full of "lessons," I actually had notepads printed with a pharmaceutical RX on them. Silly as it seems, it forced me to look at things with a more critical eye. By writing my lessons, then my options, on a prescription pad, I began prescribing workable solutions. Meditating on those prescriptions during long walks alone and through writing in my journal, I'd release everything to my spirit power for final solution. I always suggest this practice to all my clients.

Notifying Yourself and Others If Your Focus Changes

In the 1920s, when 7-year-old Bud Lueck visited his first museum, the curator placed a rock in his hand and said, "This is over a million years old." Lueck remembers, "That's when I fell in love with the old!" Collecting relics and artifacts quickly became Lueck's obsession, as did becoming a curator. In school in the middle of the Great Depression, he was advised to go into something more practical instead. "Use your abilities in math and science to make a great deal of money," Bud's counselor recommended. "Keep adding to your collections, and then build your own museum!" Eventually, that is exactly what Bud Lueck did. But, first, he collected and contributed to other museums.

By building a number of successful sheet-metal businesses, he was making the kind of money it took to purchase the beautiful items he wanted to collect. Specializing in artifacts from North America and South America, Lueck and his wife traveled the length and breadth of the continent over the years, purchasing and collecting artifacts illustrating prehistoric artisans' skill in everything from chipping flint to pottery and basket-making, from decorative feather to beadwork. One large collection he was able to purchase once belonged to well-known collector Daddy Stanley. All the time, Lueck's businesses continued growing, aided by the invention of a copper drain designed especially for flat industrial roofs. Then, more than 40 years after he'd begun collecting and donating items to other museums, his vision changed.

Reevaluating where he was—and where he was going—Lueck decided to stop donating to other museums and build his own. In 1993, Bud's revised dream came true: Grossmont/Cuyamaca College District, 17 miles inland from San Diego, California, donated a prime piece of land for his use. With additional financial help from his adult children, friends, and community supporters, the spectacular Heritage of the America's Museum opened on January 20, 1993.

Not only were four wings necessary to house his collection, but the building itself was designed by Lueck. Inside, all of the display cabinets are also his handiwork. Outside, surrounded by palms—grown from seedlings by the Luecks—today the museum is host to busloads of children—some of whom for the first time get to hold a million-year-old rock in their small hands.

Is the museum worth all the time, money, and planning? Is it worth the years of propositions made and denied? Worth the setbacks and disappointments?

"Absolutely," says Lueck. "There were times when I ran into obstacles and they set me back a day or two—maybe a month. But I never lost sight of where I was going." So, trusting that—some day—his museum would be a reality, Lueck convinced others to believe in his dream by continuing to collect, plan, travel, and study. Persistence over five decades paid off, not just in the long run, but all along the way. Bud's enthusiasm captured the interest of his wife, his children, and grandchildren, too. As for the community, it now has a treasure right in the neighborhood, both in the collections and in Bud and Bernadette, too, because they are in the museum six days a week, leading tours.

So, share any change in attitude or direction with those on your empowerment team, your friends, and the community at large. By notifying them, you receive the encouragement that you might need to keep going. Just as you can't build museums without the help of others, you can't be a change agent if you are too busy doing what you've done before!

To keep a close check on yourself, step back and observe where you are right now. Write down answers in your journal to the following:

❖ *How many times have I altered my biggest dream, or my focus, since I began reading this book and writing in my workbook?*

❖ *Have I claimed the changes for myself?*

❖ *Have I notified anyone of these changes?*

❖ *Do I want/need to notify them now?*

❖ *Who do I want to notify? By what method?*

❖ *How do I want them to react?*

❖ *What will I want them to do to empower me?*

Visualizing Yourself Back in the Good Times

Many recommend using creative visualization these days, and for good reason! Athletes are encouraged to "picture" themselves achieving more than they have previously thought possible. Motivational speakers often suggest to their audiences that the first step toward achievement lies in envisioning themselves doing what they've always wanted. The results of visualization are often rewarding and, sometimes, almost miraculous. Time and again, people have amazed themselves by actually accomplishing what they've previously only hoped for. If you haven't tried to picture yourself realizing and celebrating your biggest dream, don't worry that—logically—envisioning yourself to accomplishment doesn't make sense. Just know that your mind, body, and spirit are working together and can make your smallest to your biggest dream a reality. So, if you haven't been doing so all along, it's time to trust your own intentions.

You can't see what you can't see: to give physical representation to what is in your mind's eye, you're going to assemble a Destination Board to determine where you are going. Start by clipping out words and pictures from magazines and brochures to reflect what you want to acquire, achieve, and celebrate. Collect pictures or things that represent what you want to experience for mind, body, and spirit. When you are ready, glue them onto a large posterboard to create your Destination Board. Look at this often: the physical realities in the real world. They are all yours for the asking—and the working. This board becomes a visual affirmation that will remind and empower you every time you look at it.

Going Beyond Your Own Perceptions

For anyone who has difficulty working with things they can't see, measure, or weigh, I can only say that there are many things that I've never witnessed that I believe. For instance, I've never encountered an angel, yet I believe the millions who say that they have. I'm not able to wire a house, but I fully expect the dishwasher to work when I turn the knob. Look at your mental energy as something at the other end of your mental power switch. Envision it! By accepting the something out there beyond your own perception and line of sight, *you can expect* your energy to move the instant you turn it on. Use that energy to fire up your creativity, to further illuminate your path, and to incorporate your wishes into your ever-changing life.

After years of doing this, I can actually feel energy circulating within me. As the current courses through me, it carries me to the place where my ideas originate. Because I embrace that flow, there is a massive change in my energy level. If I can do it, so can every dreamer alive!

The key is to know your biggest dream, then make the commitment to use all of your own powers to bring it about. Tell others what you intend to do, and then begin doing the work! That is when the magic begins.

Once this begins, you discover that, although there will always be some sort of obstacle (a loan to secure, a computer to purchase, a language to master), earlier limits are gone. When asked how she transcends the limits of the human body while dancing, ballerina Nadia Sonenburg replied, "I let the music play *me!*" Just as sculptors say the statue already existed in the stone, artists frequently admit, "I didn't paint this picture; it was inside of me just waiting to get out." In the same way, many authors and song-writers pay homage to an indefinable something deep within them that is the source of their works. In much the same way, in-touch architects and carpenters use spatial vision to interpret what their clients' want, and mechanics sense what's wrong with engines. All transcend their training and conspicuous knowledge to tap into another dimension. From there, they can foresee the highest need and the highest good. So what are hunches, reality, and creativity but other words for miracles and magic? When energized, each becomes an aspect of your conscious commitment to yourself. Activate the magic in you by placing yourself in your biggest dream. Believe in what you created. Then get on with achieving it!

To do that, take a few minutes to join me as I return to a time of childhood belief in magic and miracles. Sit with me for a moment in the silence as I retreat inward. Then, lifting a mental wand, swoosh it around in front of you. You may discover, as I have, that suddenly you are free from having to think sequentially. In that instant it becomes all right to embrace everything that—in reality—appears illogical. No longer must your creative wondering be slowed by tried-and-true, step-by-step processes established by someone else. That is because, by returning to a state of childlike wondering, you can accept what the world regards as sleight-of-hand. Believe alchemy is possible: that an ugly toad of a person can be transformed into a handsome, loving human being, that you can manifest anything that you want. Believing in that kind of thinking that transforms you and that frees your creative spirit, generating the purity of energy you need/want to obtain a powerful shift beyond your usual view of things.

Now, by recording in your journal or drawing on your art pad, answer these questions:

✦ *What did I see?*

✦ *What did I feel?*

✧ *What else did I experience?*

✧ *Have I gained clarity on any aspect of my biggest dream?*

✧ *How will this change the way I have viewed things?*

✧ *How is this going to alter what I am doing?*

✧ *What results can I see coming from all this?*

This exercise is excellent to repeat whenever you feel discouraged or "down" when you'd rather be enthusiastic and "up."

Living Congruently With the Dream

In bad times and good, each of us needs to remind ourselves to live every day as if our dream was already realized. The world is full of people who say they want to be one thing, but act as if they want to be something else. If you want to be an executive, accept total responsibility and administer accordingly. If you want to be a minister or healer, practice behaving with the purest of intent and action every day of your life. If you want to be a politician, exemplify what public servants ought to be by living an honest, responsible life. Whatever it is you want to become, ask yourself throughout the day, *Am I at this very moment living congruently with my biggest dream and dream self?*

Combining personal power and spirit energy must be practiced from moment to moment. That means walking in your strength and wearing it for everyone to see. To illustrate, one of my favorite sayings is, "Wear the right costume, and the part plays itself." In other words, if you are to fully accept the power of what you want to become, you'll need to practice wearing the right "costume." The force of this should never be underestimated, as the following examples show.

Recently, I organized a visit to a fabulous clothing store in La Jolla, California, for a dozen men and women interested in empowering themselves so they might achieve their dreams. I'd arranged for store personnel to receive us after-hours. Also on hand were make-up artists, hairstylists, and professional dressers experienced in providing professional people with the proper clothing. When "finished," each member of the group modeled his or her new self for the rest of us. What an experience! What fun we all had as we celebrated our dream selves.

Appearances make *such* a difference: In each instance, the person emerging from the dressing room was not the same as the one who had gone in. A school secretary emerged as the polished professional she said she wanted to become. It wasn't just the hairdo, or the beautiful suit; she walked differently and held her head at a different angle. In that new suit, she was what she wanted to be.

An attorney, tired of suppressing her femininity, had exchanged her ultra-conservative, severely tailored suit for a softer, but still professionally appropriate, jacket-dress ensemble. Her previously untouched face was lightly enhanced with subdued eye shadow, blush, and lipstick. Revealed were surprisingly blue eyes and astonishing cheekbones. Would attractiveness hamper her in the courtroom? Others in the group were firm in their belief that it would not!

Out from the dressing room came a man who was there only because his wife insisted. Although all of us knew that he was employed by his wife's family, and that he hated the job, none of us knew how he dressed for the job. We had only seen him in what we assumed was after-work clothing: jeans, sneakers, and a sweatshirt. But the dresser, knowing his dream of becoming a college instructor, had dressed him in a tweed sports coat, khaki slacks, and loafers. It caught everyone by surprise. Just as quickly, they accepted what they saw. Their reaction solidified his determination to get an advanced degree and teach history. In a matter of minutes, he moved beyond obstacles to work on his dreams, and some of those who saw the transformation became more excited to be members of his empowerment team.

Did permanent change come to everyone that night? Interestingly, all of the men so loved wearing their new costumes that they purchased them and moved forward. It was the women who held back, unwilling—or unable—to accept responsibility for making their dreams come true. Some of them worried about what their partners would say to any changes they might make. Others worried that their partners would be upset by the cost of the clothing. In fact, two of them had become so anxious about even considering such changes that they became physically ill while trying on the clothing. But in the weeks that followed, four women processed the supportive reactions they'd received that night and went back to purchase their "costumes." What this illustrates is that the mere act of "trying on" what you'd like to become is a step in the right direction. By doing this repeatedly, you begin making your dream come true. Activate your personal and spirit power by wearing the appropriate attire. Make it a habit!

Another way to redefine an outward manifestation of your changing spirit is to update your home and workspace. First of all, get rid of everything that doesn't fit who and where you want to be. If you want an elegant life, better to serve salt from its original container than to continue to use plastic shakers. But maybe all you need is to change things around. A friend of mine found a whole new way of using what she already had by reading a book on feng shui, the ancient art of activating personal and professional power through furniture arrangement.

Simply turning her desk so that she faced the door instead of having her back to it, transformed the energy of her office. Moving color around and using mirrors added to the circulation of that energy. Sound trendy? Many corporations hire feng shui experts to assist in their planning and arrange their environments. If they're investing in activating "alternate" energies, why can't you? If, however, you can't afford to make any big changes, cut out photos of the house, furnishings, or office you dream and plan to have one day. Collect other pictures that further clarify what you want and add to your Destination Board, or keep a file, so you will have when you are ready for that dream step.

The same goes for your automobile. Sell it and buy another, paint your present car, visit a car parts store to purchase emblems of the car you plan to buy when your dream is realized. Glue them in their proper place on the old buggy, restore the chrome, buy a new license plate holder, change your route to and from work, and/or begin shopping at different stores. Each small outer conversion reflects the inner changes you are making to live compatibly with your dream.

It is difficult to manifest your dream unless you've moved beyond all that has held you back. By activating personal and spirit power, by using your creative energy by working for the highest good of all involved, and by dedicating yourself to becoming the very best that you can be, you find yourself aligned with your destiny, in a life that suddenly becomes simpler. That's because, with your commitment to realizing your biggest dream energizing everything you are doing, you are no longer afraid of anything or anyone. So, whether you have fully identified your biggest dream, recognize only part of it, or are moving forward in response to an inner feeling about it, let's celebrate what you've accomplished in the *real* world of dreamers and dreams.

Never Again

No longer afraid to reach for your dream, never again will you allow the "real" world to lower the curtain on it, or you. By always aligning with the highest in life, you place yourself among life's celebrants. When journaling about what it means to live your life and your dream consistently and simultaneously, consider the concept that these two realities really merge. It's not as if you have to live your life and your dream separately. Quite the contrary: The two are uniquely intertwined to create your own special place in the world.

With everything you've learned about yourself and the real world, you are ready to move beyond anything that does not directly affect the realization of your dream. Describe and record all the components of your life that you are no longer willing to allow affect your dream.

_____

_____

_____

_____

_____

_____

_____

_____

_____

_____

_____

_____

_____

_____

_____

_____

_____

_____

_____

_____

_____

_____

_____

_____

_____

In Chapter 1, you wrote your story of the things you wanted in your life. Now, go back and cross off everything that is no longer congruent. Add whatever you are now ready to include.

Make the Dream Real...Make it Yours

Living your dream in the real world now becomes natural. Each and every experience becomes significant as you travel within your own adventure.

How do you notice that there is really no clear distinction between the "real" world and your dream? In what ways does it feel wonderful and second-nature to fill your day with your dreamwork?

_____

_____

_____

_____

_____

_____

_____

_____

_____

_____

_____

_____

_____

_____

_____

_____

_____

_____

_____

_____

_____

Rejoice!

You have made many new and bountiful changes in yourself. By living congruently with your claimed reality, you
are continuously activating and celebrating all your dreams.

6

Celebrating Your Dreams

When was the last time you celebrated, really celebrated, someone's birthday, a friend getting a new job, or a big change in your own life? At which of those celebrations did you achieve the highest state of merry-making? Is it possible that there is an even higher state?

Celebrating each forward movement—no matter how small or seemingly insignificant—opens the door to becoming increasingly in touch with spiritual and physical fulfillment. Eventually, you find yourself living each day of your life in a state of celebration.

"But," you might say, "wanting to live constantly in celebration is not only unrealistic, it's frivolous—even superficial. Anyway, who has the time? And, wouldn't celebrating all the time sap your energy for enjoying completion of the big stuff?" Well, it depends upon what you consider to be acts and states of celebration. From Eastern philosophies we have learned that it is desirable to live in the now—to be present, right now, wherever we are. Many people have removed themselves so much from being present in the moment that all they can do is project, plan, collect, and deal with "musts" around them. This is often obvious in those retirees who can't accept that "someday" has finally arrived and find it terrifying to actually spend the money they've saved. Those who are younger often need to just as consciously get beyond time and money limitations by rediscovering, then redefining, themselves even without the security of tomorrow. Does that mean that you should cancel your insurance and stop investing for the years ahead? Emphatically not! I'm inviting and reminding you that it is essential for your inner growth to not get so caught up in preparing for tomorrow that you lose today.

How Have You Celebrated up to Now?

As a child, the mere act of splashing paint on paper was one sort of celebration. Having it hung on the refrigerator was another. Many dreamers find a release of great joy in creating, although their art may not be gallery quality and their poetry may be enjoyed or seen only by themselves. What such creativity provides is renewal, pleasure, and accomplishment. *Notice and remember* these moments in your life.

Think back to the last time your threw a really terrific party, planned a special event, shared a precious moment, purchased a gift for someone who did not expect it, or rejoiced in someone else's accomplishment or success. Each of those were a celebration!

Make a list of those occasions that filled you with joy or a sense of fulfillment or satisfaction. Describe for yourself how each was celebrated, and the feelings you experienced. Determine what brought you into those elevated states of excitement. How long did it last? A minute or two? An hour? Weeks? Months? Years? In thinking and writing about those occasions, noting how you felt afterward, and the duration of those feelings, you capture what you've learned from those experiences. To get you started, consider these:

✧ *Birthdays.*

✧ *Holidays.*

✧ *First touchdowns/home runs/baskets.*

✧ *Passing a test.*

✧ *Starting of menses.*

✧ *Getting a driver's license.*

✧ *Graduations.*

✧ *First sexual experiences.*

✧ *Marriage.*

✧ *The birth of a child.*

✧ *Promotions.*

✧ *An original idea or creation.*

❖ *Recognition for having made a contribution.*

❖ *Unacknowledged contributions.*

❖ *Being a member of a team.*

❖ *Religious ceremonies.*

❖ *Life transitions.*

❖ *A problem solved.*

❖ *Recovery from illness or addiction.*

When asked about ways in which such occasions, events, and passages have been celebrated, people come up with some really simple means of acknowledgment: telling jokes, singing in the shower, playing music extra loud, buying an ice-cream cone, or writing a poem, as my client Lissa did:

I SING A SONG OF CELEBRATION

I sing of sunsets, silly hats

Somber moments, midnight chats

Walks on beaches and in parks

Oohs and aahs for wolves and sharks

Flickering candles, wedding bells

Laughter, love, and magic spells.

★ ★ ★ ★ ★

Others write about celebration in different ways:

Celebrating means a gleeful party with lots of balloons. It's the sparkle, the pageantry, the Christmas, the birthdays.

★ ★ ★ ★ ★

I have daringly gone ahead and intuitively done what I thought necessary. Sometimes I have spent lots of time alone, whether painful or joyous, to really feel what I needed to do to take the next step in my dreams. I have talked to others, read, sang, danced my wishes, my downfalls, and my progress, alone and with others. I have reminded myself to be true to myself and not only push ahead, but to surrender to the moment.

★ ★ ★ ★ ★

I believe that women must bring celebration to everything they do each day. There is life to celebrate when we cook, garden, nurse our babies, play with poor children, and decorate our homes.

★ ★ ★ ★ ★

Enjoying the moment with no worry about the past or future, and sharing that joy with others.

★ ★ ★ ★ ★

I have celebrated my dreams by journaling to help me sort and plan for what I want, telling only positive people about my dreams instead of worriers or negative people who just act like dreams are for story books or TV.

★ ★ ★ ★ ★

I have listened to the stories from the lips of others; I have listened to the stories that the animals tell, the birds, the trees, the whispering grasses. I have dutifully taken them down, drawn them into my heart, and then released them into the world to fly forth in freedom, to find new homes in the hearts and minds of others. Even a stone can speak in the arms of a stream! It is all a great celebration of life and living!

★ ★ ★ ★ ★

I walked the breadth of Prospect Park, Brooklyn, just breathing in the evergreens.

★ ★ ★ ★ ★

Celebration to me includes events, joyful experiences marking a specific issue, life milestone, or giving meaning and significance to the beginning and ending of one of life's transitions. But in the bigger sense, celebration is more than an event: it is an attitude; a joyful approach to all of life. Being able to embrace and experience authentically the whole range of feelings. Being fully alive. Accepting with enthusiasm where I am moment to moment. Celebration is my commitment to life and living.

★ ★ ★ ★ ★

Privately, I dance inside! The realization of dreams for me has become an internal thing. It's not about recognition from anyone; it's about feeling at peace and being happy with my own true center!

★ ★ ★ ★ ★

Do you recall Myra, the woman whose house and life were in total disorder? Well, five years later, Myra has not only achieved all of the goals she first established, but she has become a happier, more fulfilled person. In her own words you can see the change available to anyone willing to work toward being the most of who they can be. Myra is a shining example of what happens when you identify a dream, work unceasingly toward its accomplishment, and learn how to celebrate each step along the way.

The word *celebration* brings to mind past parties and reunions, lively activities involving family and friends, all which required lots of preparation and considerable work. But celebration today means something very different to me. More and more, I'm finding a way of rejoicing that does not include lots of people. It is a new sense of freedom; an aloneness accompanied by excitement, fear, and change. It is a solo celebration—an adventure into me and who I am. In other words, I celebrate what is important to me in a powerful, quieter way. Now I appreciate simpler pleasures, like those reflected in a smile or kind word, a gentleness and caring heart, a shared intimacy with my children.

★ ★ ★ ★ ★

Look back at what you've discovered so far about your own celebrations, habits, and experiences. What did your celebrations have in common? How were they different? What are your talents as a celebrator? What celebrating skills have you developed? What objects and activities help to trigger your celebration memories and recreate the spirit? Write a summary in your journal of what you have learned about the ways in which you celebrate.

Write about where you are now versus where you want to be in four months, in six months, in a year, in five years. Share those ideas with your empowerment team and dream coach. Discuss all implications. Then, having done all this, write a short paragraph summarizing your thoughts on an index card. Post the card on the dashboard of your car, on a mirror, or some other prominent place where you will notice it often. As the days go by, observe your reactions to seeing it: Are your ideas on celebration expanding from day to day? As they do, you will need to reflect this by altering, or adding to, your card. In fact, you will probably want to write a new card (or cards!).

Soaring in the New Dimension: The Fireworks Begin!

Having examined your own feelings toward personal achievement and celebration, do you better understand the reward/gratification processes you have already established for yourself? It is through understanding them that you further actuate your dreams. As a dream activator, you operate in a new dimension: By following your mission, you rocket into the realm of the extraordinary. Even there, however, negative influences from outside can affect you if you allow them to. To protect yourself from doubt and opposition, program your inner spirit each night to awaken you each morning caught up in the wonder and hope of your dreams. Throughout each day, if needed, call upon that energetic exuberance to renew you.

Having done so much to define and claim your biggest dream, you've embraced more power than you suspected was available. Encouraged to identify your own personal kinds of celebration, you now find that it's time to integrate what you've learned.

Take time right now to dust off your mental ribbons, balloons, and sparklers while you are getting out your favorite pens, and begin to write in your journal; today is the day your words take on a special shine, so describe what you are feeling and thinking. Write to declare the new you!

It is said that the only mind you can ever change is your own. However, you know better than most that as you alter your thinking and doing, everything and everyone around you changes, too! Unity minister and author Emmet Fox describes the method of building a "mental equivalent" as the means by which a person, community, or nation achieves innermost desires. Once again, for dream activators to get what is wanted, they must create a mental equivalent of themselves living and celebrating their dreams.

Answer the next set of questions to forever change your life. As you take the time to think, write about, review, change, answer, and discuss the first 16 questions with your empowerment team or dream coach, you are becoming more specific in building the mental equivalent of what it is you want to celebrate.

1. What is the biggest dream you want to celebrate in this lifetime?

2. What is your passion?

3. What is it that you know you were born to do?

4. How do you know that you were born to celebrate your biggest dream?

5. In what ways does your biggest dream involve celebration?

6. How will celebrating your biggest dream impact you and the universe?

7. What do you need to do to realize and celebrate your biggest dream?

8. What do you want to do to realize and celebrate your biggest dream?

9. What do you choose to do to realize and celebrate your biggest dream?

10. What are your opportunities/challenges for growth?

11. Why is realizing and celebrating this dream important to you?

12. Did you use any excuses today? What were they? In what ways did they serve you?

13. In which ways, today, have you acted in accordance with what you say you want?

14. Who taught you to claim your biggest dream? Who taught you to accept your personal power? Your spirit energy? What do your answers suggest to you now?

15. Are you, right now, modeling the behavior of a person accepting his or her power and celebrating his or her biggest dream? If yes, how? If no, why not?

16. How did you accept your power today and celebrate your biggest dream?

Over the next week or two, consider the following:

17. *If you had just arrived on this planet and your job was to teach others to celebrate their biggest dream, what would you teach them? And how would you plan to teach them?*

Having answered the first 17 questions, devote at least a week to thinking about, writing, and discussing the last four:

18. *As a practicing celebrant, what evidence do you want each day that you are claiming and celebrating your biggest dream?*

19. *Think ahead to when you attain your biggest dream. Write the questions you will be asked by television and radio interviewers on celebration. What is your answer to each question?*

20. *Catch yourself being joyful. Every day for at least a week (or for the rest of your life), write about the following: What do you feel like celebrating? What have you thought about celebrating? What did you celebrate? With whom? How did you feel about the celebration process?*

21. *What are 100 smaller dreams that will empower you to realize your ultimate dream? When you're finished listing them, reread your list and put a star next to those you are truly committed to doing.*

When you are finished answering all 21 questions, reread and highlight what you want to consider in more depth. Copy questions or directives that you want to think and write about for further review. Draw stars next to or circle those you want to activate or enact right now. Each day, write one of them on a card and take it with you so that you can think about it off and on during the day.

To make these active reminders a part of your everyday life, carry them on your person (proximity to skin generates a kind of mental osmosis). So carry them in a pocket, pin them on clothing, or tuck them in your underwear. For the fun of it, have a phrase or sentence printed on a T-shirt. (But print it upside down so you can read it.) Let your lists and notes change, and remember to frequently update them as you and your dreams evolve. Celebrate your growth! Then, because you will soon have many opportunities to ignite the next stage of celebration, review your activators often. Write new answers to the previous 21 questions to reflect each new turn of your thinking. As you grow in awareness you will experience an inner sense of celebration of renewal of your spirit power. You will also express yourself more freely and appear more powerful.

However, along with your increasing freedom come reminders of what may have been new boundaries just weeks ago: the importance of always being honest and above-board about your intent, and achieving your goals only through shared personal and spirit power. Only then, when the perimeters of appropriate behavior are honored, does your own freedom grow. Because real empowerment comes with the inner peace that tells you that you are pursuing your biggest dream in harmony with the universe, you know that you can fulfill yourself. Continue living the following rules to establish boundaries that will establish a permanent state of independence and increasing incidents of joy.

- ✰ Live from your biggest dream every moment of every day.

- ✰ Live from the excitement of knowing that every life experience is a learning experience.

- ✰ Live from the perspective of discovery.

- ✰ Live by embracing the change that comes with clarity.

- ✰ Live from telling your highest truth.

- ✰ Live from your highest universal self each moment of every day.

- ✰ Live for, from, and in your passion.

- ✰ Live from knowing what you were born to do.

- ✰ Live from the values, habits, beliefs, and actuators that are in alignment with the realization of your biggest dream.

- ✰ Live in the purest expression of your personal power and spirit energy.

- ✰ Live from knowing everything in your life is an opportunity to use those powers.

- ✰ Live to celebrate liberating and using your powers well!

Establishing and Staying in the Now

I love that my clients say to me, "I am so glad that when we are together you focus completely upon me." By that, they mean that I re-member what they've said in the past and connect that information with what they are saying in the now. That is because I do not allow my personal issues, professional challenges, or other clients' work intrude upon the time I am spending with the client-of-the-moment. However,

I believe that before any of us can do this we must learn to live in the now. By that I mean to start to notice how you behave when something happens that makes you happy. Because our reactions are usually spontaneous, we don't give them their due. Catch yourself smiling, singing, whistling, or humming and recognize that these actions are reflections of inner joy. Then go back to what prompted the smiles and whistles to discover what it is that you are celebrating: a task done well, a dream step accomplished, rain after a dry spell, a child's pleasure, a beautiful sunset, a bouquet of freshly cut flowers, learning a new skill, empowering another dreamer, volunteering for an organization that you believe in, or the sense of power as you wake up each day knowing you are truly committed to your biggest dream.

Starting right now, practice noticing and recording commonplace events or situations that produce mini-celebrations. This habit of being aware will bring you into the state of celebrating your dreams!

Recently, I was on my way into my local library. On either side of the walk are rows of well-tended rose bushes. The bright blooms filled me with a sense of well-being. Then as I walked up the steps, one particular flower caught my attention. Maybe it was the delicacy of its color, or the darker hue rimming the outer edge of its petals that captivated me. At any rate, I stopped, leaned down to smell it, and then studied it carefully. "Thank you," I whispered, "for enriching my life." Then, aware of the way my spirit had embraced the beauty of that flower, I continued on into the library with an inner sense of joy of being in the right place at the right time—part of my dream, because when I'm in my right place, I affect and inspire those around me.

Benefiting Others

What wonderful, perfectly *normal* thing grabbed your attention yesterday? Your children cheerfully squabbling over morning cereal? Be glad that they are alive and healthy, and know that their freedom to agree or disagree reflects your acceptance of them as children. When you are in your right place, they are too! Celebrate that! In the same way, celebrate your orderly in and out baskets: how wonderful to see the day's tasks so clearly delineated so that you have time to concentrate upon your biggest dream. Celebrate having tasks or chores that allow your mind to run free, that benefit those close to you, and that provide time for you to contemplate your next dream steps!

One of the more pleasant benefits of my having written my *Live Your Dream* series has been receiving a newly published book by another author. Inside, on the title page, she had written a beautiful thank you, because it was through reading my book and doing the writing exercises that she had realized her dream of authoring her own book. Who wouldn't celebrate that? And who wouldn't celebrate hearing from a young woman who'd gone from writing poetry for herself to writing for a local newspaper to leaving a message that she'd just won the San Diego, California Press Club Award for the best non-daily article of the year? Just recently, I attended the opening of a private art gallery where I was publicly acknowledged by the owner as providing the structure for realizing his dream. Celebrate? Oh yes, I celebrate all the time! Do you?

Take time out right now to list what it is around you that brings you pleasure and into a sense of celebration. Then reread each item and add the feelings you recall while experiencing it.

Simply by consciously recognizing that which is nurturing and pleasurable to you, you elevate yourself into a state of celebration.

Make a list of experiences and feelings you might never have considered celebrating before. One that you may want to include is being alone. Just think about celebrating being all by yourself. Then think of the relaxation that comes with nothingness. Isn't it lulling to do nothing? And doesn't having nothing to do or think or be sometimes refuel you so that you can get back to something productive or meaningful? Try investigating the words sad, excited, and fearful. When your list is completed, review how far you have come from your initial reaction to seeing those experiences and feelings written in words. Next, note how each of those feelings and attitudes empower you as you move forward into your biggest dream.

Celebrating the Passion of Life

Remember a time when you went through the process of celebrating but felt something was missing. Maybe you attended an event or party where people were supposed to be rejoicing but you detected no real spirit of camaraderie or joy. And you noticed that because everyone was only pretending, they drank a little too much and laughed a bit too hard to make up for the loss. In that company, instead of experiencing real thrill and jubilation, you ended up being uncomfortable because you left feeling depleted rather than energized.

In your journal, record what wasn't there, or was wrong. If you could go back and change anything, what would it be?

Now remember events that you have wholeheartedly celebrated. For instance, how do you act when your favorite team wins? How do you feel? What do you experience when watching the perfection of a dancer's leap, the perfect stroke of an artist's brush, the first frost of the year, the changing colors of migratory birds, a baby's first smile? Is your exhilaration at witnessing these occurrences not a form of celebration?

Not all celebrations are felt with the same intensity or duration; appreciating the fleeting beauty of a rose, for instance, may not compare with the lifelong thrill of having won a Pulitzer. We can increase our awareness of prizing the everyday ordinariness of human achievement, for each carries us forward in awareness, and with awareness we draw closer to our biggest dream. How many times have you experienced the excitement that comes in doing something well, the elation that accompanies a memorable sunrise, or the enchantment of an unfolding new love? How many times after those experiences were you uplifted simply by remembering? By acknowledging and retaining the joys of the past, we produce and celebrate them again and again. Prior thrills encourage us to anticipate future joys of our own making. Let's move ahead by projecting those "high" feelings you will experience upon the achievement of each of your dreams. Imagine yourself at the head of a grand parade; envision being applauded, celebrated, thanked, or honored by your peers. How do you feel?

"Wait a minute!" you say. "To attain and maintain such a high-energy state implies a revolution in the customary way the world works." How true! Without problems to focus on, what would the world's citizenry think about? What would there be for any of us to do? Would we just sit around all day, daydreaming or watching TV? Would we take lots of walks and meet friends to chat about our dreams? Without crime, wars, starvation, and homelessness, would life become less focused or less meaningful? Or is it possible that those things continue to exist because, subconsciously, most of us fear that without them we would be left with nothing to do? Not to those of us working on our dreams. Not to those of us taking time to celebrate the process! You might be interested in what some dream activators have discovered as they worked toward realizing their dreams. People from many walks of life have shared their notions of celebration with me. Here are some of their replies:

Celebration means joyful living, breathing out with as much love and joy, and taking in with as much excitement and energy as every cell of your body can hold.

★ ★ ★ ★

It means being alive and awake and noticing what is happening around me. It means actually acknowledging the good instead of just taking it for granted. It means living in the awareness that life is *marvelous* and that I am showered with blessings every day. It means being grateful for what I have, which also happens to tell the universe to keep sending more!

★ ★ ★ ★

To me, celebration is being open and willing to listen and learn, to move and keep moving, to have complete trust as I travel along the path toward a new beginning. "The joy, joy, joy, joy down in my heart; down to my heart to stay." Celebration is appreciated.

★ ★ ★ ★

Openness! Life! Music! Laughter! Connection!

★ ★ ★ ★

Living in celebration means a lot to me because it makes my life simplified and happier.

★ ★ ★ ★

Celebration means that I embrace my life with love, joy, and serenity. I rejoice in other's accomplishments, and my own.

★ ★ ★ ★

Celebration means to be fully present, knowing the "all-rightedness" and love in each moment. Celebration is to be at one with each and every moment, breathing it in, breathing it out. Being responsive with all that I am, and all that I have to give.

★ ★ ★ ★

Celebration is an unconditional, euphoric participation in life.

★ ★ ★ ★

Celebration, to me, is doing the work that passion generates, and that generates passion.

★ ★ ★ ★

I'm continually lost in an evanescent fog, trying some new technical challenge, hoping to discover some marvelous combination to soothe my insatiable curiosity. To find people who respond to my work with, "Look, someone has said what I could not say; someone has made sense of this part of my life"—now that's living in celebration!

★ ★ ★ ★

Celebration means to praise God every day for all the special talents, abilities, and potential He gave me.

★ ★ ★ ★

Celebration is a daily conversation with God—about all the best in His universe.

★ ★ ★ ★

Feeling joyous, deserving of that joy, taking time to notice and mark accomplishments. It is thriving, not merely surviving.

★ ★ ★ ★

The way rainy days make me smile.

★ ★ ★ ★

Warm breezes on summer nights.

★ ★ ★ ★

Your best friend answers your question and you haven't even asked it yet.

★ ★ ★ ★

Spending times with friends and family.

A whole day in bed reading a good book.

Watching any birth.

Mourning those who have passed.

Simply life in all its forms.

Sharing my art skills with others; helping children see God and creation through art, helping mentally challenged people develop skills that will be helpful in several ways, giving the elderly activities to be excited about. I also believe I celebrate through prayer, meditation, creating art, and thanksgiving.

Feeling with my whole body.

Celebration to me is sharing my joy in being alive, aware, and present, physically and spiritually. It means daring to say honestly what I feel in my deepest heart needs to be said to people individually and to society in order to promote growth, hope, and evolution.

Celebration means honoring and validating the experiences of our lives.

Celebration is like a dance: You are happy, free-flowing. Celebration is reverence and honor. Celebration is gratitude, the dance of appreciation and thanks.

★ ★ ★ ★ ★

Thornton Wilder in the play *Our Town* speaks through one of his characters: "Oh Earth, you are so wonderful. Do any human beings ever realize life while they live it, every minute?" To me, true celebration occurs when we are fully alive and celebrating each moment, each breath of life. My work in hospice has brought a profound change to my life. I am learning to let go and open myself more and more as I sit with those facing the ultimate surrender of letting go. I have lived a very rich life, full of intense joys and deep, painful sorrows. Now I see that all that has brought me to his place at this time. As Dag Hammarskjold pointed out, celebration can be summed up in the words: "For all that has been, thanks. For all that will be, yes!"

★ ★ ★ ★ ★

Celebration to me means to join my voice with the other voices in this world to make a joyful noise!

★ ★ ★ ★ ★

Giving Yourself Permission to Trust and Commit

By embracing the decision to face and triumph over any challenge, you unleash everything within you that cries out for expression. In other words, you are transformed! In one quantum leap, you find that the work you've committed yourself to do is no longer cumbersome. Instead, it is cause for rejoicing, because in doing it you can more fully express the love, compassion, creativity, beauty, truth, and wisdom that is at the center of what you want to accomplish. And so you celebrate. Every day, you consciously appreciate that which carries you forward, that which makes the journey more fulfilling. Soon, celebration is a habit. You aren't there quite yet, you say. Instead, you are constantly called back to the world's reality because you must live from paycheck to paycheck, or because you remain in a "bad" relationship, or because you haven't yet found the "right" job! Well, if you are living for Fridays and vacations, take a closer look at what you are, and are not, doing to move forward.

Get out your journal, pick up your pen, and write answers to the following questions:

✧ *What am I living* from *and* to?

✧ *Where would I rather be?*

✧ *What would I rather be doing/having?*

✧ *Do I* want *to live in the celebration of my biggest dream? Why?*

✧ *On a scale of 1 (struggling to survive) to 10 (expansive celebration), where do I place myself right now?*

✧ *Am I living from choices or reactions?*

✧ *Am I living in my spirit energy?*

✧ *Am I living in my personal power?*

✧ *Am I living in joy?*

✧ *What beginning/action do I want to take to prepare for more celebration?*

✧ *What regular action will I take to practice* living in *celebration?*

Let me tell you about some of the celebrations that followed having done this exercise. Many people gave themselves permission to get married, have children, start businesses, leave jobs, work through old hurts to heal their wounds, go back to college or acquire further training, volunteer for charitable work, and realign with their deepest dream selves. Each of them has stopped saying, "Someday, I'll..." and is now setting aside time each day to embrace and celebrate all that is in his or her life.

Celebrating at Work

I have often found too few people who are including consistent celebration in their present work-a-day world. Perhaps they are surrounded by others who see joy in working as frivolous—as if those who are happy while working are not really serious about their jobs. As they see it, "serious" workers look forward to the end of the workday. Any rejoicing they do is reserved for after the workday is over. For many, celebrating is something to be waited for, like a party, a special night out, or a vacation. Certainly, it is not something they do every day, all day long. From their point of view, there must be a significant, socially acceptable reason to celebrate. Just as unfortunate, that type of person views celebration as something done to acknowledge what people do instead of what they are, limiting them to take notice of measurable accomplishments made on the job, or the years spent doing it. Don't be limited by people who see celebration as coming from outside themselves, as an external reward. Remember: As you change, so do those around you. One of my clients did this very simply: Each week she placed a piece of her valuable crystal collection on top of an office cabinet. Even in the muted light of fluorescent lighting, the crystal facets flung twinkles of light around the room. Amazingly, even this small physical change in the environment evoked attitudinal changes. So change your attitude and start spreading your light.

Another example of on-the-job attitude is Rick, a bistro manager, who revels each day in meeting vacationers who regularly stop by for a meal or a latte. With them, he celebrates his memories of experiences he's had in their states or countries. Every day, he does this. It's a successful bistro and a dream come true!

Celebrating in Times of Loss and Sorrow

How do you celebrate when you've just lost your job? When your latest attempt at realizing a dream has "failed"? Or when there has been a loss, death, or disaster in the family? You:

   ✯   Acknowledge all of your feelings about the situation.

   ✯   Acknowledge everyone else's feelings.

   ✯   Allow yourself time to grieve a loss.

   ✯   Allow others their grief and fears.

   ✯   Meditate, journal, or pray to keep your connection with your inner spirit strong.

   ✯   Step aside and reevaluate where you are in your life.

   ✯   Reevaluate your biggest dream. How will the loss affect it?

   ✯   Know that you are still in charge of pursuing and realizing your dreams.

   ✯   Design a time frame in which you can move on through the pain and confusion to continue your life and your journey to your biggest dream.

   ✯   Select the specific steps you will take to begin, follow through, and reach your biggest dream.

These are the "rules" that I followed when I lost many of the physical things people ordinarily think of as necessary. I accepted the reality and fully embraced the learning as part of my journey. In times of difficulty, I have learned to look for things to celebrate. In fact, I look for what I call *cause to celebrate* all the time. Do you?

Knowing When and What to Celebrate

Remember a time when you went through the motions of celebrating and felt something was missing. What wasn't there? Or was it that something was actually wrong? Family celebrations often fall into this category. Although you are glad that cousin Amy found such a perfect life and new husband, you'd also like something of your very own to celebrate. Added to your discomfort is the fact that everyone else is trying not to upset Aunt Marie by mentioning her recently deceased husband. Although she says nothing, when no one remarks upon how much he would have enjoyed the wedding, she is hurt. Around her, everyone keeps pretending that all is well. When the wedding reception is over, each feels an underlying sadness, a sense that something important has been left undone or unsaid. Everyone consoles him or herself by getting back to "normal," but "normal" all too often means accepting or pretending that everything is all right. But not you.

Having come this far in your development, you know that feeling loss after a celebration is not what you choose. You also know that if you are not celebrating little things every day, you are still accepting the restrictive standards of those around you. This is the time when dream activators go back and review their responses to the list of nots that tie them in knots. Recall the person you were before you accepted any restrictions. Enjoy once again the thrill and joy of being carefree and experiencing all the new things the world offered. Be 2 years old again and inspect all the new stuff around you. Remember yourself at 3, climbing anything and questioning everything. Do all those things again and again, until you've moved beyond the restrictions that might still be holding you in bondage!

Knowing Who to Celebrate With

Throughout this book I have referred to the importance of having support and an empowerment team. Since the first edition of this series I have created a Web site (*www.joycechapman.com*) to provide information about my services and to invite dreamers to join with me to celebrate and claim their dreams. One of the pages of the Web site is dedicated to dreamers just like you who are ready and excited about claiming and celebrating their dreams. I call this section a *Dream Circle*. I have also designed a guidebook to help dreamers create a structure for forming their own circles. (The guidebook is included in the latest edition of the *Celebrate Your Dream!* companion workbook for those of you who know the value of surrounding yourself with dream activators to empower you and join to assist in many ways to empower others.)

In most of life, it is always easier to follow in another person's path or walk with someone else as you accomplish or set out towards a goal. There is nothing more unsettling than to think, *Am I the only one who thinks this way?* or to feel that certain loneliness of marching along without anyone else in sight.

You might ask: *Why be in a Dream Circle?*

These are some of the reasons to form a Dream Circle. When you discover some of your own reasons, I hope that you'll add your ideas and write and share them with me.

✹ To free your energy and be creative!

✹ To state the dream—the biggest dream—you are ready to claim.

✹ To commit yourself.

✹ To share with other dreamers and join together for fun and support.

✹ To join with other dream activators.

✹ To step into your power and celebrate the life of your dreams.

✹ To ignite your spirit power.

✹ To practice making celebration a habit in your life.

✹ To declare that this is the day, the month, the year to make your dreams real!

✹ To live true to yourself and fulfill your destiny.

Why should you form or join a Dream Circle? For one reason: *you.*

A Dream Circle supports you and your dreams by joining your dream to others. When we actively acknowledge our dreams by sharing them with others, we say to ourselves and to the world,

"I have a dream.

I am claiming my dream.

My dream will come true!"

I encourage you to discover the wonder and power of a Dream Circle. It empowers you and your dreams and brings fellow dreamers together.

Celebrating Celebration

Now that you have come this far, take full measure of yourself. What do you, as a powerful celebrant, look like? How are you expressing yourself? What is your biggest dream? Who are the people you choose to spend time with, work with, dream with, and celebrate daily experiences with? What do you value about them? What do they value about you? What do they say they like best about you? Which of their statements do you most appreciate? Whenever you are asked about your biggest dream or the current dream you are working towards, what is your reply? Do you suspect that it might one day be different or even bigger?

What are the character traits you most value in yourself? Do you radiate your purpose to others? What new activities do you enjoy? Why? Which activities do you commit yourself to because they support your biggest dream? Which parts of your current dreamwork are going to require more money? Yours or someone else's? What else do you spend money on? Why? Are all your daily habits and practices congruent with your biggest dream? What legacy do you want to leave?

Write an imaginary news magazine story describing you and your full use of personal power in celebrating your ultimate dream. In this way, celebration becomes a lifestyle. Reread this often, always updating it as your world expands. And remember: Celebration is simply an attitude, a way of living every day of your life!

Thinking Personally, Acting Globally

We've all heard the expression "think global, act local." I believe that it forces each of us to accept personal responsibility for saving the world when we turn that around to "think local, act global." Every drop of water we squander, each aluminum can we throw way, and everything we consume eventually affects the rest of the world. The same is true of our dreams. By activating our own powers to make our dreams come true, we change our families, neighborhoods, cities, the world, and ourselves. When enough of us are engaged in celebrating our fulfillment, we can revitalize life in every corner and byway of the planet. So use your powers to fulfill your biggest dream. Become even stronger by combining your power with that of other dream activators. For those of you ready to work together to save our world, I invite you to share your dream scripts with others and join in the reformation of consciousness and accomplishment. And keep your biggest dream alive by celebrating everything in life every day. I believe it all matters!

Never Again

Never again will you question whether or not to celebrate every step, every experience, every wish, hope, and dream realized. You are now choosing to live your biggest dream in the state of celebration.

Take time to record the most jubilant life experiences that you have truly celebrated.

_____

_____

_____

_____

_____

_____

_____

_____

_____

_____

_____

_____

_____

_____

_____

_____

_____

_____

_____

_____

_____

_____

As a celebrated dream activator, you are growing increasingly aware of every choice each moment of your day. Become dedicated to enhancing your daily journey by recording the everyday celebrations.

Make the Dream Real...Make it Yours

Working toward a dream is at times fun and exhilarating, despite challenges to your forward movement. Reaching a dream requires dedication, persistence, and acceptance of one's own power. It isn't always easy, but aren't you glad that you are doing it?

List that which has shown you how to act in your moments of rejoicing and celebrating.

_____

_____

_____

_____

_____

_____

_____

_____

_____

_____

_____

_____

_____

_____

_____

_____

_____

_____

_____

_____

_____

_____

_____

_____

Describe your life and the people who will be with you in spirit or body at the moment of your rejoicing and celebration!

_____

_____

_____

_____

_____

_____

_____

_____

_____

_____

_____

_____

_____

_____

_____

_____

_____

_____

_____

_____

_____

_____

_____

_____

_____

_____

_____

_____

_____

Celebrate!

You've created your own style of living your life in celebration. By doing that, you've made living your biggest dream a reality. You celebrate your life, those who support and empower you, and your biggest dream!

Index

About the Author

Joyce **Chapman** is a dream coach dedicated to living true to herself and her dreams and inspiring others to do the same. She offers a home-study program for individuals who want the guidance of an expert as his or her dreams become more exciting and challenging. For those individuals who want to use the step-by-step program presented in this book and become part of an international dream team to facilitate and coach, she offers a training and certification program.

In addition to *Celebrate Your Dream* and *Celebrate Your Dream Workbook,* Joyce is author of *Live Your Dream: Discover and Achieve Your Life Purpose, The Live Your Dream Workbook: Discover and Live The Life of Your Dreams, Journaling For Joy: Writing Your Way to Personal Growth and Freedom, Journaling For Joy: Writing Your Way to Personal Growth and Freedom* (the workbook)*, If I Had Three Wishes the Only One Would Be…:Your Personalized Plan for Discovering Your Life Goals, Igniting Your Spirit Power, and Making Your Dreams Come Alive,* and *If I Had Three Wishes the Only One Would Be…Your Personalized Plan for Discovering Your Life Goals , Igniting Your Spirit Power, and Making Your Dreams Come Alive* (the workbook).

Joyce Chapman, M.A.'s professional background includes 18 years as a teacher and teacher trainer in the California public school system and two years as founder/director for an innovative private school. She has a master's degree in counseling psychology. She is well known as a pioneer in the field of personal and professional coaching. Her intention is to create and design programs that will enrich and empower the lives of her readers, clients, and workshop participants until the end of her life.

She is also extremely proud to share her life wishes, hopes, and dreams as a wife, mother of four grown children, grandmother of 11 grandchildren, and friend who treasures friendship.

For more information, you may contact Joyce at:

PMB#111

826 Orange Avenue

Coronado, CA 92118

www.joycechapman.com.

—